Trapstar 3

Blake
Karrington

This is a work of fiction. All of the characters, organizations, and events portrayed in this novel are either products of the author's imagination or are used fictitiously. Any resemblance to actual persons, living or dead is purely coincidental.

Chapter 1

Brandon awoke to the feeling he had dreamed of so many times since the first day he met Brianna Campbell. Seeing her lying there in the bed and feeling her in his arms is what life was supposed to be. He pulled her warm body closer to his. Her body was so soft; he began to trace the contour of her waistline with his equally soft hands. His fingers ran up and down her back before settling both hands on her soft ass and giving it a squeeze. *It's Bounty soft.* He laughed to himself and continued to massage her backside as the tip of his tongue stroked her right ear with soft wet licks. Blood rushed up from the bottom of his genitals to the shaft of his dick; he was ready.

Brianna had been trying to play sleep, knowing she had to be up soon for what she knew was going to be a long day. But Brandon had found her spot right behind her earlobe and she could feel the creamy liquid building between her legs. She moved her butt further back into his body and began to grind against his hard dick. Brandon smiled, knowing that he had her full cooperation now. He ran his fingers through her hair and turned her face towards him. His soft warm tongue slid gracefully into her mouth. Brianna caught it and sucked on it gently. She was glad that both of them were late night teeth brushers, or this would have been out the question for her. She turned towards Brandon's flawlessly chiseled chest. Brianna went straight for his nipples and began to suck and lick them vigorously.

Brandon guided his body down until his face rested between her legs. Brianna was straddling his face, with her arms and head resting on the large California King sized headboard. He placed his arms under her soft thighs to gain full access to her clit. He licked and slurped her wet juices, enjoying the sweet tart taste of her nectar. Brandon would switch from long soft licks, to short hard licks, with a sucking motion. He drew the ABCs, just like the Kama Sutra book had instructed. From Brianna's reaction, it was working. Her body moved in a circular motion as she continued to grind to the music Brandon's tongue was making. The feeling was driving her crazy, and the first orgasm was quickly approaching. She was trying to masquerade it, in hopes that it would not come too soon, but to no avail. Her thighs began to tighten around his head and she could feel the lump in her throat growing as her body began to spasm.

The loud sound of her phone going off was enough distraction to delay the orgasm. She had read in a magazine that if you placed your phone in a glass before bed, it would heighten the sound of the alarm and ringer. Because she was such a hard sleeper, Brianna used this method to ensure that she would not miss anything important. She reached over to hit the ignore button, in hopes that the call wouldn't interrupt her and Brandon's morning love session. He was still feasting on her pussy and she was sure that she could catch her place again with just a little more concentration. However, when she looked down at the screen, she knew that this was not a call she could ignore. It was Charrise, and with the recent events and her delicate psyche, Brianna had to answer.

"Hey sis, what's going on?" Brianna asked, nearly out of breath.

Hearing those words, Brandon stopped his oral assault. He knew the whole mood was about to change. Lately, anything dealing with Brianna's family brought a solemn tone with it, especially when it came to Charrise. Since her attack, Brianna had not left her side, except for short visits with him. Brianna had attended all of Charrise's doctor visits, and one day when Brianna ran into the corner convenience store, Brandon had observed the nearly twenty thousand dollar dental bill Brianna had paid for Charrise's oral surgery and new veneers. Although Brandon understood the sisterly bond, he had to admit he was somewhat jealous of the relationship and time the girls shared.

"Turn the TV on Channel 9 and call me back afterwards." Charrise answered and hung up.

Brianna grabbed the remote and punched in 09.

"Good morning. Our top story of the morning is the trial of Levi "Cowboy" Parsons, the man who was charged in the gruesome triple homicide four months ago on the west side of Charlotte. Tommy Torrez for Fox News is at the courthouse with the latest." The news anchor reported before the camera cut live to the courthouse.

"Thank you, Debbie. Today, both the prosecution and defense will be wrapping up final jury selection in this possible death penalty case. Police and prosecutors allege that Mr. Parsons is a career criminal, who back in April of this year went on a killing spree, leaving three men dead. One of whom was a police informant. We will keep you up to date on the latest, as more information comes in. Now back to you, Debbie."

Brianna turned the TV off. She knew this day was coming, but it didn't make it any less emotional. Her father had unexpectedly come back into her life, and now he could be taken away. She laid back down and placed the pillow over her head. She wanted to cry, but she knew she couldn't because she had to be strong.

Chapter 2

Eagle read the article about the Fed's sweep of North Carolina's drug kingpins. He shook his head as the lead investigator smiled like a Cheshire cat at him from the front page of the newspaper. He and Niya had not been allowed to communicate with each other since their arrests. He had spoken to Flash, one of his runners on the street, who told him all he knew was that Niya had been sentenced. He couldn't get any more information than that.

The chatter of the common area died down. The energy of the room shifted and caused Eagle to look up from his paper. An attractive older man sat down at one of the gray tables. He wore a designer suit, and shoes. A guard stood beside him speaking with another guard. The man looked at Eagle with a steely gaze.

"That is one cold ass motherfucker right there," one of the inmates said as he and another inmate sat down at a table beside Eagle. "That nigga is that old school kind of gangsta. You heard what he did, right? That dude took out bout ten to fifteen niggas by himself."

Eagle listened to the inmate's obviously inflated story and shook his head.

"That is why that nigga is called Cowboy. Cause if you going in with him... it'll be like the old west. Shit, he a legend in these streets," the other inmate said as he sipped his water.

Eagle looked back at Cowboy and made eye contact. Eagle had not seen him in a few months, since he and Niya had hooked up. He had hoped to see him at his grandmother's house when he took Niya to visit her, but his grandmother had told him that Cowboy had not been by in about a week. Growing up, Eagle had become accustomed to not seeing his father for weeks, even months at a time. Cowboy and Eagle's mother were two of the east coast's most vicious hired guns.

The guard tapped Cowboy's shoulder. Cowboy stood then nodded to Eagle and followed the guard out the door. Eagle took a deep breath, his mother was now six feet deep in the ground, and his father was just six feet in front of him. He sat back and inhaled as he thought of his grandmother, Maggie. She would be taken care of financially always, but he knew it was going to break her heart that the two men she loved more than anything in the world were now back in the prison system.

Charrise and Selena were still gazing up at the large 50 inch plasma TV hanging on the wall over the fireplace. They had seen the Channel 9 report, and had switched the channel only to see that Channel 3 was covering the case as well. They both listened attentively to the words that followed.

"Well, Chanel, today is the jury selection in this case. The District Attorney, along with counsel for the defendant are expected to wrap things up by tomorrow afternoon. We were told that this case will be tried as a death penalty case, and District Attorney Larry White seemed to confirm this in a press conference by simply saying, "We are seeking the maximum sentence."

Charrise covered her still partially wired mouth in shock while Selena walked over and grabbed the remote control off the glass table. "Damn, that's fucked up." Selena said, turning the TV off. "These crackers down here don't play no games," she continued, as she walked over and took a seat on the sofa next to Charrise.

No one thought that it was going to get this bad for Cowboy, especially since they really didn't have a lot of evidence. Cowboy had only made one statement when he was arrested. "Hello, I want my lawyer." He was a true soldier who knew the system well enough to be its worthy adversary. The lead investigators knew that they were not dealing with some young dope boy. If they wanted to build a case against Cowboy, they were going to have to work at it the old fashioned way... by investigating.

Charrise stared at the television, but she didn't hear or see anything on the screen.

Selena looked at her friend whose once slim petite frame had filled out to a curvy plus size one. It was a significant amount of weight gain, but Charrise seemed to be comfortable with the size. Selena watched as Charrise placed the straw in the glass and sipped her water. Her eyes reminded her of one of the zombies from the movie they had watched the other night.

Charrise continued to stare at the black screen.

Selena stood and touched Charrise's shoulder, which made her jump.

"Hey! Hey girl! You okay?" Selena said, squeezing her shoulder.

"Huh?" Oh damn girl, I was in a zone just now." Charrise uttered, grabbing her chest. "Damn you scared the shit out of me."

"Yeah, I see." Selena said, forcing a smile.

The crew knew that Charrise was violated when she was kidnapped. No one pressured her to talk about the incident because she was seeking help through counseling. Her going to therapy gave Brianna confidence that she would get through this, because Charrise had recognized that she needed help and was seeking it.

Selena felt helpless because she wanted to be there for Charrise, but she just couldn't find a way through the wall that Charrise had emotionally and mentally constructed. She kind of felt guilty for being angry at her friend for talking to a damn stranger about what happened, rather than the family that was right there for her. Feeling helpless was not something that Selena was accustomed to, and seeing her friend in so much pain was heartbreaking. Even worse was the fact that the fools who had caused the pain were six feet deep, so there was no one else left to punish. *So I need to focus my anger on being supportive for my girl,* she thought to herself.

Charrise stood up and stretched. "I'm good, girl… just got a lot on my mind. You ready to take me to see Dr. Rice? I need to go put some clothes on." Charrise's mouth was moving, but her eyes were still empty.

Selena opened her phone and found her favorite picture of the entire group. The girl that smiled at her from the picture may have somewhat physically been there, but her spirit had been broken or completely destroyed. Selena hoped that she would snap out of it soon.

"Y'all niggas ready or what?" Jonathon asked as he cocked a bullet into the chamber of his thirty-two shot Tech 9mm. Neither Kevin nor A.J. said a single word. They both checked their guns to make sure that they were locked and loaded. Simultaneously, everybody pulled the cloth ski masks down over their faces and exited the car. In broad daylight, all three men walked down Main Street, guns in hand, not caring about the few people who were standing outside on the small street.

"Keep y'all eyes open," Jonathon advised as he counted the number of people sitting on porches and standing around the house where they were heading. The people who were outside stood in shock as the men walked down the street. They couldn't believe what was going on. Until now, this was considered to be one of the quiet streets in the neighborhood.

"Pick up the pace!" Jonathon yelled out, noticing that a couple of people standing outside had gone into their homes.

The male and the female that were sitting outside in front of the house was oblivious to Jonathan and his boys approaching. It wasn't until the female noticed that the noise on the street had become silent, that she turned to see what was going on. The male friend she had with her also turned to look, but by then, A.J. had a gun in their faces.

Jonathan and Kevin wasted no time walking up the steps right past them. Jonathan checked the door to find that it was locked, and instead of asking the male or female to open the door, he took one step back and damn near kicked the door off its hinges. Jonathan and Kevin rushed into the house like they just graduated from Navy Seal training. Two men sat on the couch in the living room bagging up dope on a glass table while a single female stood in the kitchen stuffing money into the money machine.

Kevin swiftly made his way to the kitchen, keeping the young female at gunpoint while Jonathan secured the two men on the couch.

"Keep ya hands where I can see them, lay face down on the floor." Jonathan instructed the two men in a calm voice. "We're not here to hurt nobody, we just want the dope and the money," he told the men as he disarmed them.

Kevin made the female in the kitchen lay down on the ground with her hands on top of her head. He wasn't even worried about the couple of thousand dollars that was on the table. What he came for was more than that. He tucked his weapon into his waist, grabbed the back of the stove with both hands, and flipped it on its front.

"Hurry up my nigga!" Jonathan yelled from the front room.

Kevin ripped the floor tile up to see the latch that opened the floorboard door. It was locked when he tried to pull it open, but he quickly remembered that the key was in the top right corner, in back of the stove taped to the metal plate. Once he got the floorboard door open, he reached in and pulled out a black book bag, and then a blue small duffle bag. He didn't even have to look into it to know what was in them, and it would have been a waste of valuable time to do so. He simply threw both of the bags over his shoulder and darted to the front of the house.

Seeing that, Jonathan rolled both of the men over onto their backs and fired several shots into their knee caps. They yelled out in pain as the bullets ripped through their legs. Jonathan needed to be sure that neither one of them would try to get up and follow them.

"Let's move!" Jonathan yelled as he backed out of the house.

A.J. and Kevin began walking off immediately. The young female and the male that was outside in front of the house were laid out flat on their stomachs at the bottom of the steps. The woman in the kitchen watched and waited for Kevin and Jonathan to leave the house before she jumped to her feet. She ran over to the kitchen table, reached under it and grabbed the Mossberg pump strapped to the leg. She cocked a slug into the chamber before running to the front of the house.

"Weak ass niggas," she mumbled, looking down at the two workers whining and holding onto their knees.

She kicked open the screen door just in time to see Jonathan and his boys getting into the car. She ran down to the bottom of the stairs, raising the pump and catching it with her free hand. The first round that she let off didn't do much damage considering the distance between her and the car. The small pellets hit Jonathan's car, but it was just enough to get everybody's attention.

"Oh shit," Kevin yelled, seeing the female slowly walking towards the car while letting off round after round.

Jonathan started the car, but the closer the female got, the more damage the pellets did.

"I got dis bitch." A.J. said, rolling out of the back door.

A.J. and the female exchanged fire, but the female was the first to run out of slugs. A.J. kept firing, trying his best to take her head off. She dropped the pump and jumped behind a tree for cover.

"Let's go!" Jonathan yelled to A.J., who quickly jumped back into the back seat.

Instead of going down the block and having to pass the house, Jonathan threw the car in reverse then backed down the block at a high speed. By the time the young female peeked her head from around the tree, the black Caprice classic was out of sight.

Chapter 3

Eight out of twelve jurors had been selected in Cowboy's murder trial so far. Each and every one of them were old and white, and each looked like they had experience with making nooses for nigga's necks. *This is a jury of my peers?* Cowboy laughed to himself. He was black and Muslim, shit they may as well stick the needle in his arm right there in the courtroom with this jury. He thought back to seeing his son. He had hoped that Eagle would have followed a different path from him and his mother. The young dude was tough, and unlike many of the young niggas out there, Eagle was smart. Cowboy had no idea what Eagle was locked up for, since the guards wouldn't allow them to make contact, but Cowboy was going to make sure he got whatever he needed.

He stood and smiled at Brianna.

"I love you, Dad. Keep ya head up." Brianna said as the Sheriffs took him out of the courtroom.

Brianna had grown closer to her father over the last few months. Although he was in a lot of trouble, Brianna needed him more than she ever thought before. He was her biological father, and they had missed so much time together. She was determined to do everything she could to get him out of this mess. A mess that was her fault. She grabbed her bag and began leaving the courtroom.

"Brianna!" Mr. Casteno, Cowboy's lawyer sprinted to catch up with her before she walked through the doors.

"Yeah, what's up, Casteno?" Brianna said as she put on her Chanel sunglasses.

"I know you and Mr. Parson find the jury to be a little odd, and are wondering why I don't have any African Americans selected, but you gotta trust me on this." Casteno said as he pushed the glass door open for Brianna. "My team and I are the best in the state, and we are going to do everything in our power to get your father a not guilty verdict." Casteno said, touching her arm while looking into Brianna's eyes. "I just want to reassure you that we will do everything to get the most desirable results."

Brianna forced a smile. Casteno had been her deceased boyfriend, Tre's lawyer. He was right, he and his team managed to work magic for Tre through his many cases. She knew that he would work hard at making sure Cowboy's case would be handled with the same diligence as Tre's cases.

"I know you will, Casteno. I will see you in the morning. I gotta run." Brianna said as she ran down the steps of the courthouse. She waved and continued towards the parking garage.

Charrise splashed water on her face as she leaned over the sink in the restroom of Dr. Rice's office. She inhaled and looked at herself in the mirror. With each session, the memories of what happened to her in that house with those animals resurfaced. Dr. Rice told her not to be afraid to remember, and she promised that as they began to return, it would be easier for her to work through the trauma. She had advised the doctor that earlier in the day, she had flashes of Tank eating her pussy and Duke forcing her to suck his dick. As she began to describe the flashback, Charrise became ill and ran to the restroom. There was a light knock at the door.

"Charrise, are you okay? Can I come in?" Dr. Rice asked.

Charrise opened the door.

Dr. Rice smiled at her and walked inside. Dr. Rice wore her hair in a large auburn afro, which today, she allowed to flow loose. She wore a soft orange cotton tank top and brown flare legged pants with orange open toe Chanel pumps. Dr. Rice sat on the small beige bench that was beside the sink and touched Charrise's hand. "Just take deep breaths, and when you are ready, we can continue."

"No, I think I have had enough for today. I don't think I can talk about this anymore." Charrise turned and opened the door. She walked down the narrow hallway that led back to Dr. Rice's therapy room. The smell of fresh roses filled the room, and the dark turquoise and blue painted walls reminded Charissse of the Caribbean. She sat on the large dark blue leather couch.

Dr. Rice sat in the turquoise large wing back chair that sat ninety degrees from the couch. Charrise knew that everything in this room had been thought out, and served a purpose with its position. She had taken three semesters of psychology courses when she was in college, and she had enjoyed them. Ironically, she did not enjoy being one of those case studies she had read about.

"Charrise, you have my card. I am available to you anytime. Please don't be afraid to call or text me." Dr. Rice said as she handed Charrise another business card. "This time, don't put it in one of those designer bags and lose it." Dr. Rice laughed.

"You're good, Doc."

"I do get paid for knowing people." Dr. Rice joked. Charrise grabbed her small Coach Sling bag. Dr. Rice walked her to the door and touched her arm. "You have fifteen minutes left."

Charrise smiled. "I just need to process what we talked about already, Dr. Rice, but I will cash in those fifteen minutes during another session." She hugged her, and for a moment, she felt a twinge of electricity run through her body while she embraced the doctor.

As Charrise began to pull away, she kissed Dr. Rice on the cheek. Charrise felt her face become warm and she walked quickly towards the large wooden door that lead to the outside. "What the hell did I do that for?" She mumbled to herself as she walked down the stairs.

Selena was sitting on the bench reading a book on her Kindle. "Hey girl you ready to go?" Selena said as she closed the cover.

"Yeah, I am starving. Can we get something to eat?" Charrise said, looking back at Dr. Rice's office. It was located in South Charlotte, which had beautiful flowers blooming this time of year. Charrise was grateful that the heat had not hit its max yet, because it was a beautiful spring day.

"Okay, but we got to grab it to go. You know I have to pick my cousin, Chatima, up from the airport today. We can shoot by Porter's Grill and grab something right quick." Selena said, putting her Kindle in her Michael Kors tote.

"Just forget it. You go do whatever you got to do, and I will just walk." Charrise sighed and began walking down the sidewalk.

Selena trotted to catch up with her. "What is wrong with you? Damn. I told you I would take you, and you already knew about Chatima coming." Selena said while touching the base of her neck.

Charrise stopped at the crosswalk and waited for the light to change. The light changed and she walked quickly across the street.

Selena could hear her breathing heavily as she walked. "Charrise! Charrise! Damn it girl!" Selena said grabbing her arm.

Charrise tried to pull away from Selena. "Let go!" Charrise said, fighting back tears.

"No, not until you tell me what the fuck is going on with you. Damn, I thought therapy was supposed to be helping your ass, but every time you come out of that damn place, you seem even more on edge. I am not letting go of you until you tell me what the hell is wrong. I'm your girl and family, what the fuck can you tell some stranger that you can't tell me and Brianna?"

Charrise's shoulders dropped and Selena loosened her grip. They started walking back towards the parking area.

"Charrise, I know that you went through hell, but I feel like you pulling farther and farther away from us. Please talk to me. I love you, girl, and I want my sister back." Selena stared at Charrise, hoping her words were penetrating her heart. "Charrise?" Selena said with her voice breaking.

"I'm four months pregnant, Selena."

Selena felt her body temperature drop as if someone had poured a pitcher of ice-cold water over her. Charrise made eye contact with her for a brief moment. Selena exhaled and took Charrise's hands. She had no comforting words to say to her friend. She now understood her behavior and the weight gain. She was pregnant by one of the animals that had raped her. Selena fought back the tears and tried to force a smile. She knew her little sister needed her strong funny side at that moment.

"Well, that would explain why you have gone from Jada Pinkett to Jill Scott, honey!" They both laughed while tears formed in their eyes. "Now let's get you some food!" Selena said. Wiping tears from her eyes, she squeezed Charrise's hand. "Hey babe, you know whatever you decide, I got you. You don't have to go through this alone. We are sisters."

She kissed Charrise's hands. Charrise exhaled and was surprised at how telling Selena had made her feel mentally lighter. Now it was time to tell Brianna, and Charrise wasn't looking forward to that task.

Chapter 4

Jon, Kevin and A.J. laughed as A.J. divided the money into three stacks. Jonathan took a swig of his Sprite and checked his text messages.

"Old boy at Pull-A-Part is cool as hell. He looked like he was about to shit himself when I told him to give me $100 for that damn car." Jonathan said.

"Boy, he should have kissed your ass. That is almost a damn brand new car, and he gonna make hella money off that joint. Shit, getting them bullet holes out ain't gonna be nothing." Kevin said as he checked his watch.

"Why you keep checking your watch, my nig?" A.J. asked.

"I gotta be across town by three. I need to pick up Nina from school and take her to her appointment." The boys became quiet for a moment. Nina was Kevin's girlfriend, and she was pregnant. She informed Kevin of her pregnancy and the fact that she wasn't trying to be no one's baby mama right now. She was working on her BA and had made it clear to him that he was not the type of guy she wanted to settle for or be with on a permanent level. The words had cut Kevin deeply because he was in love with Nina. To hear that she didn't think he was good enough was hurtful. Although he didn't show it, he was upset over her wanting to kill his seed, but he felt that he had no choice but to respect her wishes.

"Yeah, well good luck with that, man." Jonathan spoke over the loud continuous ringing of the house phone.

"Jon Jon! Jon Jon! Pick up the phone!" Jonathan's girlfriend, Gator, yelled from the top of the stairs.

He got up from the table in the dining room where he, Kevin and A.J. were counting the money from the lick. If somebody was calling him on the landline instead of his cell phone, that could only mean one thing. It was somebody from his family like his mother or Brianna. They were the only two people who still used landlines.

"Yo, what's up?" Jonathan said, picking up the phone that was hanging by the kitchen door.

"Where you been all day? I been tryin' to call you..." Lorraine, his mother yelled into the phone. "I need you to come pick me up and take me somewhere."

"Momma, I can't do it right now," Jonathan said, looking over at all of the money on the table being counted by his boys.

"Jonathan Eugean Carter, I don't believe I just asked you a question. Now you get ya butt over here and pick me up before I am late for my appointment!" She demanded before hanging up the phone.

She didn't even give Jonathan time to deny her again, even though he wasn't going to. He loved his mother more than anyone in the world, so whenever she needed him for something, he was at her doorstep immediately. Jonathan looked down at his Audemars and saw that it was 11:00am.

Where the hell does she gotta go? He thought to himself. “Aye yo… Finish countin’ dis bread. I gotta go take care of something real quick. If I’m not back by the time y’all get done, give my money to Gator,” he told A.J.

One thing Jonathan didn’t have to worry about from the niggas in his crew was an act of disloyalty. It wasn’t that A.J. and Kevin were scared of Jonathan; it was more so that they respected him a great deal. They had a genuine love for one another and a bond that was truly unbreakable. It could have been a million dollars on that table, and in Jonathan’s absence, it still would have been broken down three ways, right down to the penny.

“Gator!” Jonathan yelled up the steps.

“Yes babe?” she answered, coming down the stairs with her Couture pajamas on and her hair tucked under a scarf.

“Yo, I am about to take my mom somewhere. Kev and A.J. gone stay here and finish counting this bread. You wanna ride wit me or stay here?” he asked, wrapping his hands around her small waist as he began to think about the first time they met.

He was starving that day, leaving the hospital from a visit with Charrise. Walking into the store, the aroma of potato wedges and fried chicken filled the air. His stomach growled as he nodded to the Asian woman behind the counter while he walked towards the drinks. He grabbed two bottles of apple juice and a bottle of orange juice. He walked back towards the grill where one of his high school classmates was working.

"Hey Jonathan, man. What's good wit you?" Mouse said as he dropped the basket of wings into the grease.

"Everything is everything, Mouse. Brah, you got it smelling something good in here and I am starving!" Jonathan spoke while placing the drinks on the counter.

"Yeah, I got you, cuz. What you want today? What classes are you taking this semester?" Mouse said as he handed a girl an order of fried pickles.

Jonathan dropped his head. He and Mouse were both A students in school, but Jonathan had postponed college after he was shot. For some reason, he couldn't focus or sit still, and it had broken his mother's heart. He had promised himself that he would re-enroll in the spring, but for right now, he had needed to get his head straight.

"Man, I took the semester off after... well you know." Jonathan said.

Mouse studied him for a minute, and then patted his shoulder. "Hey, I understand. You gotta get ya head clear then go back to taking over the world. So what ya want?"

"Give me four wings and an order of potato wedges."

Mouse nodded and walked over to the cooler.

Jonathan was checking his text messages when a warm breeze entered the store carrying a sweet smell of vanilla and coconut. He looked at the door and the darkest skinned female he had ever seen in his life walked in. She had a low-cropped hair cut with a pale pink off the shoulder linen blouse, dark denim Chanel Jeans with wide legs, and a pair of pink peep toe gator Chanel shoes. She carried a pink and blue Chanel clutch and gold tree earrings. He watched as she walked towards the cooler and the back view was just as impressive as the front; her ass was round and high. That pink was making her ebony skin glow.

"Damn, she got to be straight from the mother land. I ain't seen nobody that damn dark before. She is almost blue." Mouse said.

Jonathan shook his head. Women usually didn't make him speechless, but this ebony skinned chick was breathtaking. She grabbed a soft drink and made her way towards the grill. Jonathan tried to drop his eyes from her but he continued staring.

Mouse cleared his throat and Jonathan closed his mouth.

"Hello, how are you doing?" Mouse asked.

She smiled at him and exhaled. "I am tired, whew. Been on the road for a good minute, boo, and I am starving. What you got good?"

Jonathan noticed she did not have an accent at all, and up close, she was flawless. Mouse handed Jonathan his food. She glanced at his tray and turned her gray eyes to him.

"So is that good?" she said.

Jonathan swallowed. He had to get his swag under control. "Uh… uh yeah try one." He slid the tray of wedges over to her.

She smiled and took a wedge. "Thank you, I will." she answered. "Mmm, either I am hungry or you know what you doing with yo wedges, boy. Give me an order of those and some wings." She grabbed a napkin and smiled at Jonathan. "Thank you for the sample."

Jonathan stared at her for another moment. "You are one beautiful woman," he said, and immediately felt his face burn.

She laughed and he dropped his head. "Well... thank you young buck! If the men in the south are like you I am going to be in trouble!"

Jonathan smiled. "My name is Jonathan, and where are you from?"

"Hi Jonathan. My name is Gator."

That response made Jonathan laugh. "Oh ok, I get it. You not going to give me your real name." Jonathan said.

"No, that is not my real name, but that is what everyone calls me."

"I gotta say that name definitely doesn't fit you." Jonathan uttered as he scanned her body.

"Oh yeah, how you know? You just met me." Gator spoke with a seductive look.

Mouse handed her order to her. "Well, it was nice meeting you, Jonathan." She turned to walk to the register.

Jonathan winked at Mouse and grabbed his food and drinks. "I will pay for the lady's." he said, handing the petite Asian woman a hundred dollar bill.

Gator smiled at him while he took his change and opened the door for her. "Well thank you again for the southern hospitality, Jonathan."

"Of course... my mama raised me right. You never said where you were from. Unless you just don't want to tell me right now, but you could tell me over dinner."

"Look at you. Going for what you want, huh? Boy I am old enough to be your mama."

Jonathan scanned her again. She couldn't be over thirty, he thought. "I doubt that, and besides, I like a mature woman." Gator laughed again and began walking towards the baby blue G63 AMG Mercedes SUV. She clicked the alarm and Jonathan opened the door for her.

"I bet you do... I bet you do." She said as she put on her Marc Jacob sunglasses and rolled the window down.

"Let me take you out and show you around town. I promise I won't bite."

"Ahh, I know how to handle puppies, boo, believe me. I ain't scared of bites." She studied him for a moment. Youngin' was fine as hell, slim waist, broad chest, and she could tell by the way he stood that he had some size between them thighs. What the fuck? She needed to blow off some steam. She handed him her business card. "Call me later and we'll see." She rolled the window back up and pulled out of the parking space.

Jonathan stood there until she waved to him as she pulled out onto the street.

It took Jonathan two days to get up the nerve to call her, and ever since then, they had been inseparable.

Gator threw her arms around his neck, breaking him from his thoughts. She leaned in and kissed him. Jonathan was so in love with her. She knew she had him sprung ever since the first day she met him. She knew he was someone she could mold into the man she wanted. It was Gator who had convinced him and his crew to start robbing niggas. She was the original brain behind all the heists, but Jonathan had proved to be a worthy student. In a short time, she felt like they could be on top of the city with her brains and his brawn.

Jonathan had never expected he would be in the street life. Shit, just a year ago he was on his way to college. After surviving five shots, he was now dating a woman at least 15 years his senior, so he now felt invincible.

"No babe, you go ahead and handle your business with your mother. I don't think I'm ready to meet your family yet... especially your mother. I know how they can be about their sons and you her only one, plus you the baby... no not today," Gator uttered with a smile.

Jonathan grabbed his keys and headed out the door, but not without grabbing one more kiss from Gator before exiting.

Lorraine walked down the steps as Jonathan pulled into the driveway. It was only a matter of time before Herman exited the house with an attitude.

Lorraine didn't even make it to the car before Herman yelled out her name.

"Where you going Lorraine?" he asked, walking up to the car.

Lorraine opened the passenger side door.

"What you didn't hear what I just said?" Herman asked, taking the passenger side door in his hand before Lorraine could close it.

"Last time I checked, I was grown, Herman. I don't have to check in with you every time I go somewhere," she responded with attitude.

Herman huffed at her and turned his attention to Jonathan, who was gripping the steering wheel so hard his hands were cramping. He looked straight ahead to avoid making eye contact with his father.

"Ahhh, if it ain't big time Jonathan," he said, looking into the car.

"What's up, Herman?" Jonathan responded, giving him the peace sign.

"Herman? Oh, so you don't call me dad anymore?"

"You gotta start acting like one first!" Jonathan shot back without even looking at him.

That statement caught Herman by surprise. "Oh, you think cause you out here living these dope boy dreams like your trifling ass sisters that you can speak to me any kind of way?"

"Herman, don't go there" Lorraine chimed in.

"Shut up woman. That's the problem now. You always talking out of place and taking up for these bad ass kids." Herman screamed, while pointing his finger in her face.

"Yo, cool da fuck out talking to my motha like that. Show some respect for a change!" Jonathan warned his father.

That was just about all Herman could take from Jonathan. He stormed around the car towards the driver side of the Charger and tried to open the door. It was locked, so all he could do was tap on the window to get him to open the door.

"Get out the car tough guy. You bad? Get on out da damn car!" Herman yelled.

"Don't pay him no mind, baby." Lorraine said, buckling her seat belt, and locking the door. "Let's just go."

"Nah. Pops got me fucked up." Jonathan responded, reaching under his seat and grabbing the .38 snub nose.

He opened the door and got out of the car with the gun down by his side. Jonathan was still recovering from being shot, so he knew he could not handle a physical confrontation with his old man right now. Herman was such a coward. He knew that Jonathan was not 100% and he could take him out easily. One punch would probably take him down in his current state. Herman was a disrespectful piece of shit. Jonathan had stood by long enough watching him being cruel and mean to the women in his family. He was sick of his shit, and today he was going to shut his punk ass down.

"Oh, you really must have lost ya mind, boy." Herman said while looking down at the gun in Jonathan's hand.

Herman took a step forward, but stopped when he saw Jonathan clutch the gun tighter in his hand. The look he had in his eyes told Herman that his son was willing and ready to shoot him.

"I am not the same timid little boy I was five months ago. You can't talk to me or my mom any kind of way you want. Those days are—"

"I can talk to my wife any kind of fuckin' way I want!" Herman said as he took a step forward. "That damn bullet must have your mind fucked up, and I am going to remind you of your place, boy!" As he charged towards him, Jonathan grabbed him by his shirt and jammed the .38 into his mouth. The gun broke the thin skin of his inner lip, causing Herman's mouth to bleed.

"Jonathan, you stop it right now!" Lorraine yelled out.

Herman's eyes grew wide as a 50-cent piece looking up at the empty stare that his son was giving him. Jonathan blanked out for a moment because he couldn't hear the pleas from his mom. Lorraine had jumped out the car and forced herself between her husband and son.

"That's enough, Jonathan." Lorraine said in a low firm tone.

She turned his face to hers. He blinked his eyes and slowly released Herman's shirt. As he looked into his eyes, he slowly pulled the gun out of his mouth and grabbed his shirt again. "Hear me clearly… you fuckin coward. You got one more time to come out yo mouth to another female in this family, and I don't care who's around... Imma blow you fuckin face off!" Jonathan pushed Herman back and he fell to the ground.

Herman sat on the ground, breathing heavy. He wiped the blood from his chin and slowly stood. He tripped as he walked backwards towards the front door of the house. He was shaking in disbelief that Jonathan had the balls to threaten his life.

Lorraine looked at Jonathan and shook her head. She knew that she needed to go help Herman with his lip because if she didn't listen to his rant, it could be worse for everyone involved. She knew he would make her evening unbearable if she didn't baby him and pretend to take his side in regard to being disrespected. She kissed Jonathan on the cheek and began walking towards the door.

"Ma, come on. You got stuff to do. He can take care of himself. It is just a busted lip." Jonathan said as he opened the passenger door.

"I will call you later, baby." Lorraine said as she came back and patted his hand. She sighed and continued back up the walkway.

Jonathan did not feel any guilt about what he had done. Ever since he found out about what happened to his sister Charrise, and that Herman was the one to set things in motion, Jonathan no longer viewed him as a father. He had sold both his daughters out, and all for money. He was a hateful, sinister bastard. Although he had liver disease, Jonathan knew the mean old snake probably wouldn't succumb to it. Jonathan knew that Herman was the type of nigga who did not let things go. He had been defeated by

Brianna for the moment, but like a snake, he was just under his rock waiting for another chance to strike. This time, when he came from under that rock, Jonathan was going to be the one to cut his head off with his Glock.

"All rise!" the clerk of the court announced as the judge entered the courtroom from out of his chambers.

Everybody in the courtroom stood. Cowboy had on a dark blue Tom Ford suit, a white oxford shirt, blue tie, and a pair of black Ferragamo's. He looked better than his lawyer, and probably every other well-dressed man in the room. He sat at the table with his right leg lapped over his left like the O.G. he was. It didn't appear that he had a worry in the world. One would never guess that he was fighting a triple homicide charge.

Opening arguments commenced, starting with the District Attorney letting the jury have it. He described the heinous nature of the crime in detail, and not leaving out the fact that Cowboy was sitting in the middle of the dead bodies with the murder weapon in his hand. The D.A. had the jury's undivided attention for over 20 minutes straight. He sounded convincing, so much so, Cowboy got a little nervous himself.

"The testimony you are about to hear is gruesome. Mr. Parsons killed three men in cold blood, and by the end of this trial, I will prove that he is guilty." the D.A. finished before sitting down at his desk.

Casteno chuckled to himself at how the D.A. had the jury in awe during his opening argument. Cowboy looked over at his lawyer and threw his eyebrow in the air. Casteno leaned over to his client and uttered a few words.

"Now watch me work." He smiled as he got up from his desk.

Cowboy watched as his lawyer fixed his tie and then walked over to the podium sitting right in front of the jury box. Every one of the jurors looked and waited for Casteno to speak.

"I have to admit that the D.A. sure knows how to put on a good show." Casteno smiled.

A couple of the jurors smiled with him. "The D.A. gave you graphic details about the murders and how bloody the crime scene was. He told you the kind of gun used in the crime, and how my client was caught with the smoking gun. From the outside looking in, I probably would think that my client was guilty. But the thing that the D.A. failed to establish was a motive. What was the reason for my client to murder three men?" Casteno asked the jury while pointing to Cowboy.

"The D.A. set this case out, wrapped it up, and presented it to you with a bow on top of it. Well, let me be the first to tell you that this District Attorney doesn't know the half about this case," Casteno went on. "For instance, do you know that my client was shot by one of the men found dead in the house and was taken to a nearby hospital right after he was arrested? Or did you know that all three men were found with guns on or near their hands or lying right next to the body?" Casteno asked, slamming his hand on the podium. "No, the District Attorney didn't share that with you. For whatever reasons, I don't know. What you can expect during this trial from me, the attorney for Mr. Levi Parsons is to get to the bottom of what went on in that house," Casteno assured before leaving the podium and walking back to his seat.

Cowboy smiled in satisfaction at the way that Casteno left a look of curiosity on the faces of the jurors. His opening statement took less than 10 minutes, but had the biggest impact on the jurors. The D.A. was even silently commending Casteno for bringing up the two issues concerning the guns and the fact that Cowboy was also shot.

"I see you're gonna earn every dollar." Brianna joked from the bench right behind Casteno and Cowboy's table.

Casteno managed to crack a small grin at Brianna, thinking about the $150,000.00 she had dropped off at his office.

Before anything else was said, the judge took the floor. He gave the jury their instructions for trial and then took the back seat. Everything else was out of his hands, and just like that... the bell rang and the fight was on.

The District Attorney had the different officers describe the crime scene they encountered when they arrived at the blood bath. Cowboy surveyed the juror's faces as the pictures were put up on the flat screen as the officers described the carnage. Casteno objected throughout some of the testimony, but Cowboy could see that the D.A. had gotten to some of the jurors by the way some of them looked at him.

"We will take a brief recess, and reconvene in twenty minutes," the judge said as he banged the gavel.

"Dis shit ain't looking good, baby girl." Cowboy said as he turned to Brianna. "These crackers is ready to put the noose in the tree right now. No offense, Casteno."

"None taken, I'm Italian." Casteno, joked trying to lighten the mood. "Listen, I know it sounds bad right now. They are describing the crime scene to get an emotional reaction out of the jury, and to have them hate whomever could have killed these folks."

"Yeah and they are hating me right now. I can see it in their faces." Cowboy said before sipping his water.

"No, all they have done is describe the scene. No one has said you caused the carnage. No witness has said that *you* did anything. All they did was describe what they found. They only said you were found at the scene, that is all." Casteno said as he checked his phone. "Look, let me work my magic." Brianna patted Cowboy's shoulder, although she had not known him very long, she loved him. He was her father, and in the short time they had gotten to know each other, he had taken her heart and filled the hole that Herman had chipped in it over the years. The hole that needed a father's love, support, and guidance.

"Hey Bri. Hey Cowboy," Selena said as she and Charrise sat beside Brianna.

"Hey girls, what took y'all so long?" Brianna asked as she kissed them each on the cheek. Charrise made eye contact with Cowboy. It was the first time since he rescued her that she had seen him. She felt guilty that she had not visited him in jail, but seeing him was painful. Each time she thought about going with Brianna, she would remember that he was one of the men who had kidnapped her in the first place. She could remember that much, and that memory prevented her from visiting him. She had moved past that, because he had saved her and Brianna's life once he figured out what has going on. She smiled weakly at him, and he nodded. Although no words were exchanged, Cowboy acknowledged her silent gratitude to him.

"So," Charrise said, reaching into her bag for a piece of gum. "How is it going? The press is painting you as some deranged psycho killer."

"So is the D.A., but to let Casteno tell it, we are winning." Cowboy huffed. "It doesn't matter what they say or how this works out. I know I did the right thing in my heart, and that is all that matters."

Before Charrise could respond, the bailiff yelled, "All rise!"

Cowboy stood as the judge entered the courtroom. Charrise looked at the man who until a few months ago was a stranger who had risked his life to save her and her sister. Now he was willing to give up his freedom for them.

She leaned forward and whispered to Casteno. "Here." Charrise said, handing Casteno her number. "Call me after court today."

Casteno nodded and took the paper.

Charrise got up and exited the courtroom.

Brianna looked at Selena, and then back at the swinging door that Charrise had just walked through. She leaned over to Selena. "What is she doing?"

"I don't know. Let me go check on her." Selena said, grabbing her bag.

Brianna wanted to go after them, but the state called the next witness to the stand. She needed to be there for Cowboy, and she didn't want to miss any testimony.

Chapter 5

Herman sipped the warm tea through a straw as he stared out the window that over looked his backyard. His mouth was killing him. He opened the bottle of 800mg Motrin and popped two in his mouth. What the hell was happening? The tides in the family had changed, and the fucking inmates were running the asylum. Damn kids done lost their damn minds. Lorraine wasn't listening to him like she was supposed to, and this little nigga gonna make him suck on the barrel of a damn gun? He wasn't gonna lie to himself, Jonathan looked like he was going to pull that trigger for a minute. He had always told him, *don't draw a gun unless you're gonna pull the trigger.* He was grateful that Lorraine was there to calm the situation down.

"Herman!" Lorraine yelled as she walked into the kitchen. "I need to go downtown. Do you need anything while I'm out?"

Herman waved her away and continued looking at the fountain that stood over the body that was buried in the back yard. That fucking body was the only thing that little bitch Brianna had on him. She was trash, just like her damn daddy, but for the moment, that damn body was keeping him under her control.

"Ungrateful little hoe! I should have fucking used a clothes hanger on Lorraine and aborted the red bitch or taken her ass to one of them orphanages in the country and left her. She hasn't been nothing but trouble since the fucking day she was conceived." He thought aloud.

Brianna stood in the mirror and ran her hands over her black two-piece Prada skirt suit. She wore a yellow satin halter, and a pair of black Jimmy Choo peep toe heels. She had her hair pulled in a bun on top of her head, with Chinese bangs.

"Charrise?" Brianna yelled as she came out of her room into the hallway. "Charrise, you ready?" Brianna knocked on the door and then walked into Charrise's room. Charrise was snoring lightly under the covers. Brianna laughed and shook her gently as she sat down on the bed.

"Hey boo, you coming today?"

Charrise stretched then rose up. She had told herself after breakfast she was just going to lay down for a couple of minutes. She jumped up and walked to the bathroom. Brianna noticed for the first time the thickness in her hips and her waist. The shirt she wore rose up on her belly, exposing stretch marks, and her once toned behind jiggled when she walked. Brianna had never seen Charrise allow herself to fall into this kind of state.

"So how is therapy?" Brianna asked as she walked into the bathroom and sat on the toilet.

"It's cool." Charrise said as she brushed her teeth. As she was brushing, her mouth began to fill up with water and she vomited in the sink.

Brianna grabbed a wash cloth out of the linen closet and handed it to her.

"So how far along are you?" Brianna asked as she moved from in front of the toilet to allow Charrise to pee. Charrise wiped her face with the washcloth as she sat on the stool.

Brianna sat on the edge of the tub and crossed her legs.

"Umm Bri... I am trying to use the bathroom, can you leave? I need a moment."

"Girl please, I done see you shit before." Brianna said. "So again, how far along are you?"

Charrise wiped herself and washed her hands. "Four months, Bri." she said, trying to fight another round of nausea.

"So why ain't you tell me?" Brianna said trying to choose her words carefully. She didn't want to upset her, especially knowing what she had been through. Brianna started counting the months and she felt a chill go through her body as she looked at her baby sister. "Oh Rese, tell me it's not by one of those animals that raped you?"

Charrise sat back on the toilet, placed both of her hands over her face, and began to cry.

Brianna took her into her arms and held her close. Charrise was trembling and trying to catch her breath between sobs. Listening to her sister moan had taken all the boss out of Brianna. She squeezed her has hard as she could, wishing she could choke the hurt and pain out of Charrise's body. Brianna pulled her off the toilet, onto the floor. She held her like she did when they were little and Herman had given them one of his signature whippings.

"Bri, I don't know what to do. I thought about getting an abortion, and I didn't want to tell you, especially after the hell I gave you about wanting to keep Hakeem's baby." Charrise said while driving her face deeper into Brianna's chest to hide her shame.

"Baby girl," Brianna whispered, while cupping her face in her hand so that their eyes could meet. "You know I am going to say the same thing to you that you said to me, and you know what that is."

Charrise shook her head in acknowledgment. Knowing the choice she had to make, she fell back into Brianna's arms. They held each other tightly. Charrise knew what she needed to do, and that Brianna was going to be right there with her to help her through whatever it was.

Jonathan stood in the mirror, allowing his fingers to outline the scars that were left by the bullets that had pierced his body. Gator had left early for a meeting with some old associate of hers. She was trying to unload the drugs that he and his crew had obtained in their last robbery. Although he was sure she could handle herself, he didn't like being apart from her. He would feel a searing pain rip through his body and his breath would become trapped in his lungs. His vision would become blurry every time she left. For some reason, he would always get the feeling that she wasn't coming back. He wasn't sure if it was because of the age difference, or the fact that she had confided in him that she had always been with men who had money. Whatever it was, he was having one of those insecure moments right now.

He stumbled back to his bed and lay down, he tried to take deep breaths, but each time he would inhale, he felt his chest tighten. His eyes began to burn. Shit, he felt like he was going to die. He began taking short breaths, then his chest began to loosen and expand. Time passed and he was able to take deep breaths. He kept his eyes closed until he no longer felt like he was on a boat. He placed a pillow under his head and continued to focus on his breathing.

Jonathan removed his cell phone from his pocket. Knowing that he needed to get out of the house and do something to get Gator off his mind, he called up his boys and they all agreed to grab something to eat. He picked up the remote to turn the TV off. He had been watching CNN and the Zimmerman verdict was going to be read in a few minutes. Jonathan scoffed and sighed. Dude was going to get away with it. He had murdered a black male child, and the jury did not have enough melanin on it to make a difference. He didn't have to wait to hear it.

Gator checked her lip-gloss, her hair, and then her glock.

Moonie sat beside her, playing a game on her phone and laughing. "Damn Gate, calm yo self. You sitting ova dere like this gon' be an issue. You need to relax."

"Moonie, I don't know how to relax... everything has to move like clockwork. I don't need no damn hiccups in this plan. I'm on a timeline and you know it. Geter don't need to get suspicious just yet."

"Gate, he don't even know me or nothing about me. Hell, I ain't seen yo ass in two years. I saw mo of you when I was locked up than I have since I been out. I told you I can handle that nigga if you want me to. I can be in and out." Moonie said as she played her game.

A blue H2 pulled into the parking lot of the old grocery store. Gator looked in her rear and side mirrors.

"All right, here we go... Moon put the fucking game down." Gator said, sliding her glock down the back of her jeans.

"Cousin..." Moon said touching her thigh. "Calm down. Damn, the south done melted the ice you once had in your veins. I ain't ever known your ass to be this jumpy about shit. Yo ass is making me nervous!"

The Hummer pulled beside Gator's truck, and the window slowly rolled down. A light-skinned woman with blonde and brown wavy hair smiled at her.

Gator rolled her window down and nodded.

"Gata?" the woman said with a drawl.

"Yeah." Gator said.

The woman stared at her for a moment.

Moonie leaned over. "Hey Poochie, what's going on?"

"Hey Moon, this is Gata? Damn I thought it was gonna be a nigga."

"Nah, nah dis my cousin. So what you got for me, boo?"

"Me and my man got South Carolina on lock, and a bunch of hungry ass niggas on deck. Since that damn sweep a few months ago, shit is not moving like it was before. The shit that is moving is moving on the other side of town. Shit in my spot is low quality and these fools is not feeling it. Niggas is scared of the feds right now is what is going on." Poochie said, lighting up a Black and Mild cigar.

Gator shook her head. This is what she needed to hear. The feds were no issue for her. She knew how to work around their asses. It was about how to transport, and the packaging of the delivery. It was also about keeping your army small and tight. But most of all, it was about price, and since she had Jonathan and his crew robbing, she knew she could keep prices down.

"Aight, well I got what you need and the number on it is beautiful... I'm sure you will agree. I'm gone give ya a little something extra also, so I can see what you can do with it. If everything is everything, we going to have a wonderful relationship."

Gator looked over to Moon, who opened her door and walked over to the passenger side of the Hummer. She placed the blue tote bag on the seat and closed the door. Poochie opened the bag and then looked back at Gator.

“What is this?”

Gator pulled her mirror down to check her makeup again while laughing. “That? That is the new south, boo.”

Jonathan pulled up to Barah’s Restaurant.

“Yo, what it do, brah.” Jonathan greeted Kevin, who was standing outside in front of the eatery rolling up a blunt.

“Nothing, ready to get my eat on and hear about this next lick you got for a nigga.”

“I feel you, brah, but we might as well wait for A.J. before I tell you. A nigga ain’t tryin’ to say it twice, you feel me? Just know I got something big coming, brah.” Jonathan said before looking down the street to see A.J.’s car coming down the block.

“Damn, here dat nigga go.”

The old school Chevy pulled up and parked smoothly in a parking space right across the street. Jonathan had to admit, A.J. kept his ride clean. Red candy paint, 24-inch rims, and a system you could hear from a mile away.

“I see ya boyyy,” Jonathan said, extending his hand for some dap when A.J. walked over. “Let’s take dis shit inside.” Jonathan told his boys.

“Damn, what’s good, Selena?” Jonathan said, noticing her as he and his boys entered the restaurant.

"Who is this you got with you?" A.J. chimed in, noticing the beautiful young girl sitting across the table from Selena.

"Yeah, who is that, sis?" Jonathan co-signed.

"This is my little cousin from up top, Chatima. She came down to visit for a while, and why you want to know, Jonathan? Word on the street is you like them on their way to the nursing home!" Selena, Kevin and A.J. all started to laugh.

"Damn Selena… how you know about my people? I haven't even introduced her to the fam yet. Does Bri know too?"

"Boy, you know the streets be talking. I'm not sure if she does or doesn't, but you know you better say something to her. Because if I'm hearing it, it won't be long before she hears it."

Jonathan shook his head in agreement, knowing that conversation was going to be long. Brianna and Charrise were both protective as hell about their little brother, and the fact that Gator was much older wouldn't help.

A.J. still had his sights focused on Chatima. Although he wasn't usually into thick chicks, he had to admit she was stunning, and her thickness was in all the right places.

Kevin, seeing that both of his boys were caught up in one way or another, broke the temporary silence.

"Look niggas, I'm hungry, so let's order before the line get too long"

"Yeah, why don't y'all do that and call ya sista!" She yelled to Jonathan, who was already walking away.

As they stood at the counter A.J. continued to look back at Chatima. "Damn homie... she wifey material. Look at the way she eating all proper and shit," A.J. said

"Nigga quit fronting... you looking at them titties and all that ass hanging off that chair. Talking about how she eating!" Kevin joked.

"Alright, my nigga. Leave my partna alone." Jonathan laughed as they sat down at another table. "Let's get to this official business," he said, taking a seat and flipping it around before he sat.

"Look, on some serious shit we have to make a big decision," Jonathan began. "We been takin' money for a couple of months now, but in doing so, we have come up on some dope every now and then. I never was the one to wanna sell drugs, but my babe is putting something together for us that can prove to be very lucrative for all involved."

"What about your sister?" Kevin asked, with a curious look on his face.

He knew that Brianna wouldn't be to cool with the news that Jonathan was in the dope game. That was the last thing she wanted for him. She was still under the impression that he was going off to college after the summer, so she definitely did not know anything about him running around the city sticking up niggas.

"Don't worry about her, brah... we going to have that talk, when the time is right," Jonathan answered.

"I'm not gonna lie. I'm not that big on selling drugs, homie. The money good, but it takes too long to make, plus it's more work," A.J. said, scratching the side of his face.

"I feel the same way, homie," Kevin cut in. "I mean, we be doing pretty good already, and right now, brah, I am feeling what we got going on now is good enough" he finished.

"Well, it's something for y'all to think about, but just know me and my lady got huge plans. I mean we can do what we do, but I got to be there for her also… you feel me?" Jonathan asked, making sure they all had a clear understanding.

"Brah, you know we going to be here for you and yours, no matter what. So why don't we do it like this? Whatever cash we get, we split, and whatever drugs we get, you throw us a love offering. Cool? Kevin asked while looking at both of his childhood friends.

Everybody nodded their heads in agreement. "Sounds like a plan to me, Jonathan smiled. "Now, let me fill ya'll in on this lick I got for us. Trust me, y'all gone love dis shit ..."

Chapter 6

The ride to the clinic was a quiet one. Brianna pulled into the parking lot of the women's medical center and Charrise's eyes began to fill with tears. She didn't want to abort her baby, but she knew that it would be in her best interest to do it. She thought about all of the questions and comments she made to Brianna when she was pregnant with Hakeem's baby. What if the baby came out looking just like Duke, Tank or Hakeem? Charrise honestly couldn't say that she wouldn't feel hostile towards the baby.

"Charrise, look at me..." Brianna said, looking over at her sister. "I know that this might be the hardest thing you'll ever have to do in ya life, but I want you to know that I am here for you. We gone do this together," Brianna said, now getting teary eyed herself.

"What if this is my only chance to have a baby? What if something goes wrong while I am in there?" Charrise cried out.

"Shhhhh, everything is going to be alright." Brianna told her, trying her best to comfort her sister.

She reached over and pulled Charrise into a hug. They both sat there and cried for a moment, letting it all out in the car before they got into the clinic.

"God is going to bless you with a good man who is going to love you and spoil you. Y'all are going to have a beautiful baby together. A baby that will be conceived out of love. You are going to be happy, and I promise you will be a great mother one day." Brianna assured Charrise as she held her like a mother holding her child.

The sisterly bond between the two was like no other. Through thick and thin, they were always there for each other, and at times, they were inseparable. "You think I am going to find a good man?" Charrise laughed through her cries as she tried to get herself together.

"Yeah, as soon as we blow this city, ' cause the men in Charlotte ain't shit" Brianna joked.

"Damn, ain't Brandon from Charlotte?" Charrise asked jokingly.

"No, he from Monroe, and he just grew up in Charlotte. Besides, he don't count." Brianna answered while giving her sister a playful pinch.

Charrise and Brianna took a few more minutes inside the car to gather themselves before getting out and walking into the clinic. Charrise could visualize her child being taken out of her the very moment that she walked through the door. Just like that, all the confusing feelings she had just minutes ago came rushing back to her at once.

She sat on the lobby couch looking at the magazine article about the latest reality television star's dramatic entrance into some nightclub. She had been nauseous all month, and this morning was no different. Charrise smiled at another young woman who was also sitting in the waiting area. The young girl took in a deep breath before reaching down into her tote bag, taking out a bottle of water, and gulping it down.

A tall white doctor came out of the double doors and called for the next patient. "Mrs. Graham, Denise Graham?"

Charrise was not into white men at all, but he was attractive. Dark curly hair, green eyes, and a neatly trimmed goatee. He had full lips for a white guy, and it could have been Charrise's hormones, but his cologne was intoxicating.

The young girl got up from her seat and followed the handsome doctor back through the large steel doors. Before they swung back closed, she looked back at Charrise one last time. Charrise could see the fear in the young woman's eyes.

Charrise looked down, pretending to check her text messages as she choked back tears.

Brianna looked over at her sister. "Hey, do you know her? Are you okay?" Brianna asked, noticing the exchange between Charrise and the girl.

"Yeah, I'm good. I just want this over with, and no, I don't know her."

Brianna took Charrise's hand. She knew that this was hard for her, but it needed to be done. Having this baby would not be mentally healthy for her sister, and not to mention the effect it may have on the child. This was going to be best remedy for everyone involved.

"Miss Palmer?" the petite white nurse said from the door. Charrise stood and looked at Brianna. She took a deep breath as she began her walk through the double doors.

Charrise woke up to the sound of a woman crying in one of the rooms next door to her. She was so far along in her pregnancy that she had to be put to sleep for the procedure; not that she wanted to be awake for it anyway.

The doctor walked into the recovery room with a clipboard in his hand. It was as if he knew exactly when the anesthesia was going to wear off. "Good to see you again, Ms. Palmer. I was wondering when you were going to be amongst the living again," the doctor joked. "Now as I told you before the procedure, you need to stay off your feet for a few hours. I don't know if you have someone here—"

"Yeah, my sister is here." Charrise said, cutting him off as she sat up in the bed.

The nurse walked into the room and passed Charrise a couple of big ass maxi pads that looked like they could be used to extract oil from the waters of the Gulf of Mexico. Charrise took the pads and then looked around the room for her clothes and spotted them on the floor far off in the corner.

"Now, Ms. Palmer, if you have any problems, don't hesitate to give me a call," the doctor said as he left the room.

"Doc!" Charrise called out, stopping him at the door. "I need to ask you a question and I need you to be completely honest with me," she said, looking up at him.

The doctor already knew what Charrise was about to ask him. This was the first question most concerned females would ask after getting a late term abortion.

"What was the sex of my baby?" she asked, taking in a deep breath before letting it out slowly.

"Usually when women ask this question, the answer only seems to make things more difficult," the doctor advised, trying to save Charrise from any added heartache.

"Doc, please just tell me," Charrise demanded.

She didn't even know if she was ready to hear the answer, but it was eating her up to know. She felt that the least she could do out of respect for the baby was to find out what it was. She owed him/her that at the bare minimum.

"It was a girl," the doctor informed her, and then walked out of the room.

Charrise's heart dropped into her stomach for a second, and she found it hard to breathe. The nurse had to walk over and see if she was okay. It hit her so hard that she wished the doctor had never told her. Having any kind of child was okay with the mother as long as he or she was healthy, but it was extra special when a woman carried and delivered a baby girl. Charrise held back her tears as she gathered her clothes from the chair.

The nurse just left the room, knowing that Charrise needed a little time to herself.

Once she was gone and Charrise was all alone, she dropped down to her knees in the middle of the floor and allowed her tears to flow freely.

Chapter 7

Gator took out the black duffle bag and stared at the money. She knew she had at least a hundred and fifty thousand in the bag and at least another hundred thousand in the safe deposit box at the bank in South Carolina. After getting rid of nearly all the drugs that Jonathan and his crew had taken in the last robbery, she knew she needed more to keep the new pipeline with Poochie that Moonie had setup. Checking her phone, she realized that Moonie had not texted her yet, and it was way past time for her to check in.

Gator chewed her bottom lip, hoping that Moonie had made it back to Detroit without Leo, her boyfriend, becoming too suspicious. Leo wasn't anything nice. Moonie was originally from South Carolina and had been able to come down and put the situation with Poochie together since Leo was out of town. However, she never really knew when he was going to pop back up.

Gator pulled the pink wife beater she wore up and stared at the long scar across her stomach. The scar reminded her of how Leo's temper could go from cool to a volcanic eruption in the blink of an eye. Gator and Leo had fallen out on numerous occasions, concerning the treatment of her cousin. Moonie always went back to him, and Gator knew that Moonie would cut her off before she would leave Leo totally alone. So after their altercation that left her with the scar, and Leo with two bullet holes in his chest, they both agreed to co-exist in Moonie's life, by not speaking on the other.

Her phone buzzed and she exhaled as she saw Moonie's picture flash across the screen. "You're late!" Gator said.

"Yeah, yeah my plane was delayed."

"Everything cool, you alright?"

"Girl, we cool. How we looking for the next meet? Poochie and her man been hitting me all morning, talking about they nearly out already!"

"That's what's up, you let them know I will have them straight real soon. I just got done putting together a lick for my crew, so we will be straight real soon"

"That's what's up, girlie... now what's up with this young boy of yours? You robbing the cradle now or just getting the youngin' to blow your back out every now and then?" she asked in a playful manner.

The question made Gator pause for a moment. She wasn't sure what she was doing with Jonathan anymore. When she agreed to go out with him, it was all about the sex. Lately, she had been developing feelings for him, but she wasn't sure if she was really in love with him, or if it was based on convenience. The fact that Jonathan worshiped her like no man had ever done before was probably the main reason.

"You still there?" Moonie asked, interrupting her mental dilemma.

"Yeah, I'm still here... and Moonie, to tell you the truth, I don't know what I'm doing. You know I only been in love with one man in my life. After him, I swore I would never love another again that way…"

Gator was cut off by the sound of the front door opening. She knew it had to be Jonathan coming home, so she tried to hurry Moonie off the phone.

"Well go ahead and get settled in, I'll talk to you later." Gator said before ending the call, right before Jonathan walked into the room.

"Hey love… you miss me?" Gator asked.

"You know I did, babe." he responded.

"Yeah, so what you miss about me?" she asked seductively.

"Everything."

"Everything?"

"Yeah everything, but mainly that sexy skin and ass of yours."

"Is that right?" Gator said, leaning closer to him.

"So you think you can handle this skin and ass?" She asked while rubbing her hands over the same body parts.

"I won't know until I try, but I feel sure that I'll be aight." Jonathan said before pushing Gator back onto the bed.

Just like a well-trained puppy, he took his face down right below her stomach. She looked down at him as he smiled up at her. Jonathan slid his hands over her muscular thighs. He found her underwear, and with one jerk, he pulled them down her long legs as he prepared to handle his business.

Gator gasped as she felt his tongue slide over her pulsing pearl. She raised her head up to see his long thick tongue lapping her clit. He placed her thighs on his shoulders and buried his face further between her legs. She put the bottom of her shirt into her mouth to stop herself from crying out. He sucked her clit into his mouth and twisted it to the left and right with his tongue.

Jonathan loved the way she tasted. Her moans were making his dick flex and twitch in his pants.

"Fuck!" Gator gasped as she felt her lower lips quiver. Her legs hung down Jonathan's back as he feasted on her creaming pussy. She felt her walls tighten as Jonathan slid two of his fingers inside of her. She almost screamed when her pussy exploded all over his hands and face. "Oh, Oh, uhhhh."

Jonathan smiled and slowly made his way up to her until their faces met. Gator was breathless, shaking, but she knew it was not over. She locked her legs around him and pushed him to the side, forcing him onto his back. She straddled him slightly and let the head of his dick graze her wetness. Closing her hand around his long, thick, hard dick, Gator held it steady and slid onto it. "Umm..." she whimpered as she continued to ease him inside of her.

He closed his eyes as he moaned. "Hmm, babe... Damn" Her shit was tight around his dick.

Once she had every inch inside her, she had the nerve to flex her inner muscles and squeeze his dick with her wet walls. Gator was an experienced lover, and she knew how to work every part of her body to perfection.

She lifted herself up so only the head of his dick remained inside her. Slowly, she eased back down, then up again in a steady rhythm. It felt so good to Jonathan that he knew he was about to bust. Gradually, her strokes picked up and she tossed her head back and continued to ride him like a wild horse.

"I'm cumming... I'm cumming." Johnthan yelled, but Gator continued her physical assault.

She loved the way her pussy felt when Jonathan came inside her, but beyond her feelings, she knew how it felt to him. This was one of the secret powers that she held over her young lover.

Jonathan smiled as the last drop of fluid left his body. Gator was about to stop when she realized that he was getting hard all over again. She inwardly smiled, knowing that this was also a benefit of having a young pup. He could hump all night, and she planned for them to do just that. She had to have him ready for their next big score.

Chapter 8

Brandon listened to Brianna's breathing as she lay on top of him sleeping. He traced her spine with his middle finger, loving the feeling of her skin next to his.

"Good morning." Bri said as she looked up at Brandon.

"Morning, beautiful. How did you sleep?"

"Ok, I guess," she said as she kissed his chest. "It felt good to sleep in this morning. Casteno texted me earlier saying two of the jurors were sick, so they will not have court today."

Brandon wrapped his arms around her and held her close. He knew that this trial had taken a toll on her, even if she was putting up a good front.

"Good, because we need to talk."

"Oh lord, nothing ever spoken after those words is ever good." Brianna said, sitting up.

Brandon brushed the hair out of her eyes and caressed her slender thigh. Looking at her nude body and her messy hair made his member jump. He focused on her face and what he had to say to her.

"So, I have been thinking, Bri, thinking about you and me."

"Yeah, what about me and you?" Brianna said as she kissed his chest.

"The future, Bri..." Brandon said. "Our future... have you given any thought to getting out of the game?"

Brianna stopped kissing his chest and sighed. "Come on, Brandon, don't kill my vibe this morning." She said as she got up, grabbed her robe, and sat on the side of the bed.

"Bri, I'm not trying to kill anything. I'm just trying to make sure that this life doesn't kill you. The smart successful people in your business get in and out of it. It's time to think about where you want to be in a few years. I don't want it to be the in the morgue or jail."

"Brandon, you don't understand... it is not easy to just walk away." Brianna gathered her hair into a ponytail. She had worked hard to get to where she was in the game. She had to admit the constant bloodshed and ever-looming threat of being locked up was wearing on her, but she had sacrificed so much to keep what she had. Walking away from what she had built did not seem like an option she wanted to consider at this time. Oddly enough, the meeting she had today was all about her stepping back... just not away.

"Can we talk about this later? I have a meeting today and I need to have my mind right." Brianna asked while heading to the bathroom.

She jumped in the shower, hoping that the water would wash her thoughts away. She was praying that she wouldn't run Brandon away. He was the first normal male relationship she had ever been in. Tre would always be the love of her life, but he had been her lover, father, brother, her everything, so she wasn't interested in replacing him. She just needed someone who made her happy and didn't come with drama, and Brandon was that.

When Brianna walked back into the bedroom, Brandon had fallen back to sleep. She quietly slid the white V-neck cotton t-shirt over her head and put on her jeans. She slid her feet into the Gucci gem encrusted sandals and smoothed her hair back.

She blew a kiss to Brandon's sleeping form and walked downstairs to find Charrise laid on the couch watching television. She had done nothing but watch television since they had come back from the doctor.

"Come on girl, get up. You can't lay around this house all day." Brianna said as she threw a pair of shoes on the floor in front of Charrise. "Get up. I need you to ride with me somewhere."

Charrise sighed as she sat up. She walked up the stairs, without looking at Brianna.

"Hurry up!" Brianna joked while walking into the kitchen. She grabbed a soda from the refrigerator, and sat down at the counter.

After about ten minutes, Charrise walked into the kitchen. "Ok I'm dressed, let's go. Where are we going anyway?"

"Going to handle some business. Carlos' wife is in town, and I'm setting up some new peeps so we can all fall back some." Brianna said as she opened the door. "Come on, time to get back to business." Brianna handed Charrise the glock, which she tucked in her pants.

They locked the house up and got into Brianna's truck.

"What happened to Carlos? Why he not meeting us?" Charrise asked as she buckled her seatbelt.

Brianna realized she hadn't talked business with Charrise in a long time, because mentally she wasn't there. "Well, he got into some trouble in his country and had to pull a small bid. His wife, Ana, has been holding things down. This is actually my fifth time meeting her. Trust me, you will love her... everyone calls her Auntie."

Brianna tuned the radio to WPEG and let the sounds of Drake flow through the truck. She exited the interstate and turned into the parking lot of the West Oak firing range. The sounds of guns popping off flooded the gun range where Brianna was supposed to meet up with Ana, otherwise known as Auntie. It was an outside range, so spotting Ana at a secluded section wasn't hard for Brianna to do once she entered the property. Brianna watched as Auntie emptied her clip into the target with marksman accuracy. When she dropped the clip to reload, Brianna tapped her on the shoulder.

"Hey Auntie." Brianna greeted, looking at the holes in the wooden frame about 15 yards out. "You dangerous wit that thing. I would hate to be on the other side of that." She chuckled.

"I'm sure that you know how to use one of these also," Ana said, dropping a clip out and slapping in another. "Here, show me what you got." She passed Brianna the gun.

Instead of taking it, Brianna pulled the .45 ACP from her waist. She turned towards the target, cupped the gun in both of her hands and began firing. Even in the light of day, the flames bursting from the gun was visible with every shot that she took. The wooden figure of a human body took eight rounds to the head area and two more in the chest, right by the heart.

Auntie shook her head, smiling at Brianna.

Brianna looked back over her shoulder to motion for Charrise to come so she could introduce the two of them.

"Come on over here, Auntie. There is somebody I want you to meet." She put her arms around Auntie's shoulder and walked her over to a picnic table sitting under a tree out of the sun.

Charrise sat there smiling at the two of them as they approached her. She carefully scanned the area; the range was empty except for two Spanish guys who she assumed was Auntie's security.

"Auntie, this is my sister, Charrise. Charrise, this is our aunt Ana." The two women embraced before they all sat back down and began to talk. About twenty minutes into the conversation, Charrise saw Selena and her cousin, Chatima, approaching with another unknown female.

Brianna stood up. As they got closer, she met all three with a warm embrace.

"Auntie, I want you to meet a friend of mine. Her name is Gwen. Gwen, this is the woman I was telling you about," Brianna said.

"Hi," Auntie greeted, extending her hand out to shake Gwen's.

"And you already know Selena, and this is her cousin, Chatima." Brianna introduced everyone.

The women greeted each other, and sat down at the table. Brianna needed to get right to the point.

"Auntie, I asked for this sit down for two reasons. First, because my friend here needs to get a hold of some heroin. I told her that's not what I deal with, but to keep our other business intact, I would reach out to see what you possibly could do to assist her." Since Niya had been away, the streets had been dry on heroin because Gwen had not been able to secure distribution. Although Van knew Gwen, she wasn't blood family, and it was no way she could put her girl, Inga at risk, with someone she couldn't 100% co-sign. "The second thing is to let you know we need to step the packages up, because we need a lot more product."

"So what type of volume we talking about?" Auntie asked with a smile.

The women sat there handling their business like some Fortune 500 men would, and by the end of the meet, all parties were smiling like family.

Chapter 9

After a brief conference outside in the hallway, Casteno, Brianna, and Charrise walked back into the courtroom.

"You sure you wanna go through with this?" Casteno asked Charrise one last time before he took a seat at the table.

She nodded her head in the affirmative and then took a seat right behind him. Today, the District Attorney was ending his case. He produced a lot of evidence in the trial, most of which was circumstantial, but very convincing. The most important piece of evidence was Cowboy having been found with the gun in his hand. This was the same gun that had been confirmed to have killed at least two of the men. That alone, without anything to justify the murders would definitely end in at least two guilty verdicts for murder in the first degree.

"The state of North Carolina rests." the D.A. declared after his last witness got off the stand.

"Counsel, will your client be testifying?" the judge asked Casteno.

Cowboy had the option to take the stand and tell his side of the story, but he opted not to, knowing that it would give the D.A. the green light to openly dig into his criminal background. That meant that every felony Cowboy had on his record, the D.A. could bring up and question him about the details. Cowboy could not afford that. His criminal history and felony convictions stretched a mile long. It would have taken an extra two days of trial just for the jury to hear everything.

"No, Mr. Parsons will not testify today. Although we do have an eyewitness account for what happened the day my client was arrested.

"Objection!" the D.A. shouted. "I ask that we have a sidebar," he requested.

On the sidebar, the D.A. objected to Casteno bringing forth any witnesses at this stage of the trial, when he never put any on his witness list in the beginning. Of course, Casteno argued the fact that at any point during trial, he should be able to prove his client's innocence no matter what. The judge quickly ruled in Casteno's favor, allowing Charrise to testify.

After being sworn in by the clerk, Charrise took a seat on the stand. She looked out into the quiet courtroom and instantly became nervous. It wasn't until her mother walked into the courtroom that Charrise felt a sense of ease. Lorraine took a seat right next to Brianna and directly behind Cowboy.

"Good afternoon, Ms. Palmer," Casteno began. "My first question to you is, do you know Mr. Parsons, and if you do, where do you know him from?"

"Mr. Parsons is my sister's real father. I recently just met him when he saved my life four months ago."

"Can you please explain how this man saved your life, Ms. Palmer?" Casteno said, walking from around his table and standing right next to Charrise on the stand.

Silence took over the courtroom once again.

Charrise looked around and her eyes landed on Cowboy, who was looking right back at her with a shocked look on his face. He didn't expect her to take the stand on his behalf, but not only was she testifying on his behalf, she was about to make sense and fill in many of the holes the D.A. had left open.

Once Charrise started talking, everyone in the courtroom listened attentively. Even the D.A. put his head down as Charrise testified to being kidnapped by the three men that were found dead in the house. She testified to the rape, and how she was pregnant by one of the men. Her testimony to the brutal attack had the whole courtroom wiping tears from their eyes. She even testified to the weeks of physical therapy and the months of psychotherapy she had to go through, and the struggles of her having to decide whether to abort her child. Charrise didn't hold back. She even cried herself, while giving testimony.

After about two full hours of testifying, the D.A. needed a break. "Your Honor, the State asks if we can have a short recess," the D.A. said, trying to put out the fire of Charrise's testimony.

It was like he sat there and watched Charrise single handedly dismantle his case. She turned the three men who were murdered into monsters; killing the victim card the D.A. had played the entire trial.

"Well, seeing that it's getting late in the day, and I know the State wishes to cross examine the witness, I think that it would be in everybody's best interest for us to reconvene here tomorrow morning at 9:00am." the judge said, wiping the sweat or what could have been tears from his eyes.

When Charrise got off the stand, Cowboy quietly uttered the words, "Thank you," when she walked past him.

Lorraine quickly grabbed her daughter and held her tight. They sat there in the courtroom hugging and crying, all which the jury witnessed before they exited.

Herman hurried out of the courtroom. He had followed Lorraine in hopes that she was going to visit Brianna. He had been trying to figure out where she lived for months without any luck. He was surprised when he saw her exit downtown to the courthouse. He knew something had to be up with all her recent visits downtown, but he never thought about this. His stomach turned as Charrise testified about what happened to her. As she testified, he felt cold and sick, but she had made her choice to side with that bitch. If anything, it should have taught her that being with her family, her decent side of the family, would have saved her from what happened.

Herman watched Lorraine whisper something in Cowboy's ear. He had to talk himself down to keep from walking over and choking her ass out. As the judge dismissed them for the day, he quickly left the courtroom. He needed to keep his cool and execute his plan, his plan to regain his throne in his household and family. Everyone had gotten out of pocket and they needed to learn their places again and soon.

Jonathan pulled up and parked two blocks away from Betty Ford Road. He went right to work, doing his homework on his next lick. Tagging along in the passenger side was A.J.

"Check dis shit out," Jonathan said, reaching into the backseat to grab his set of binoculars and pointing with his finger in the direction that he wanted him to look.

A.J. looked through the binoculars and saw nothing but zombies walking up and down Betty Ford Road. It looked like something out of a movie, the way dope fiends flocked to the block in packs. Looking further, A.J. could see a female standing on a porch in the middle of the block overseeing several other females standing off to the side serving the fiends their product.

"Damn, it's crack heads everywhere," A.J. said, as he continued to look through the binoculars.

"They're not crack heads. They're dope fiends, a whole 'nother ballpark." Jonathan responded.

Jonathan didn't know that much about the drug game, but his knowledge did extend to the fact of knowing that dope money was better than cocaine money. He learned that bit of information from his newfound love, Gator.

"Oh, look, look, look," Jonathan said, seeing the all-white Aston Martin Vanquish pull up to the block.

A few seconds went by before a female jumped out of the car, rocking a mini skirt, some heels, and a half cut t-shirt that showed off her stomach. The binoculars were doing their job, because A.J. could see everything down to her cute face.

"I think this bitch run dis strip. Rumor has it that the chick that owns this block, rebuilt it from the ground up after the whole block went up in flames." Jonathan schooled.

"Damn, I think I remember seeing that shit on the news a while back. A couple of people died in the fire or something like that." A.J. shot back.

"Yeah, the bitch replaced every house that burned down and then opened shop back up. I'm not sure, but I think that's her," Jonathan assumed, nodding at the female who had just got out of the Aston Martin.

"Who do hell do these bitches think they are?"

"I don't know who dese hoes think they are, but they about to find out this is a man's world." Jonathan answered, grabbing the binoculars from A.J.

"So, how you wanna do it?" A.J. asked, looking over at his partner in crime.

"We sit and wait, brah. I say a couple more days of homework should set us straight. Right now, shorty that just hopped out of the Aston Martin is the target. If she is who I think she is, trust me, she is the only one we need." Jonathan answered, looking off down the street.

The men looked at each other and then simultaneously reclined their seats as far back as they could go. This had turned into a full-fledged stake out almost instantly. In a short period of time, Jonathan had exceled with this money taking thing. Sometimes he would lay and wait for somebody for days in order to get his man. That's one of the things that made him so dangerous. He had patience, and patience was a very important key to his success.

"Herman! Herman, come on, your breakfast is ready!" Lorraine yelled as she placed the scrambled eggs on the plate. Even though she and her husband had not been seeing eye to eye, Lorraine still felt that it was her wifely duties to make sure he was fed.

Herman stumbled down the stairs. It was only 9am and he was already drunk. As he staggered to the table, she looked at him with disgust.

"Herman, really. This early? What is wrong with you?" Lorraine said as she poured a glass of orange juice.

"Shut ya fuckin mouth, woman!" he shouted as his blurred vision adjusted on her. "Now put my God damn food on the table ... right now." He burped and hiccupped.

Lorraine shook her head, walked over to the stove, and grabbed his plate. She really didn't feel like arguing with him, and she knew that's exactly what was going to happen if she said anything else about his intoxication.

"I have to go back downtown today to the social security office. I will be back in a few hours. Do you need anything?" Lorraine asked as she was putting the dishes in the sink.

When she turned around to grab some more dishes off the table, the last thing that she saw was the gold wedding band on Herman's finger.

He smacked Lorraine so hard, he knocked the spit out of her mouth and blinded her temporarily. She held onto the sink trying to get her vision back, but when she did, Herman swung at her again, this time with a closed fist. He punched Lorraine smack in her mouth. This time, knocking her to the ground and filling her mouth with blood.

"You going to see your little boyfriend?" Herman taunted with his slurred speech.

Lorraine was still on the ground letting the blood drip out of her mouth onto the floor. She could barely feel her face. It was numb all over.

"You running around, going back and forth down to that courthouse to see that muthafucka. You must have lost ya damn mind," he said, grabbing a fist full of her hair and pulling her to her feet.

"Herman... Herman...please," Lorraine uttered as he dragged her to the other room.

Lorraine was out of it. She did not have any strength at all to fight Herman back. He knocked that out of her with the closed fist punch.

"You my old lady!" he yelled, throwing her onto the couch.

He began pulling Lorraine's clothes off, starting with her pants and then her shirt. He didn't even take the time to pull off her panties. Instead, he just ripped them off from the waist.

"Herman, what... are you doin'?" Lorraine cried out, swallowing the blood that leaked into her mouth from the cut on her upper lip.

He stood over top of her and unbuckled his belt, letting his pants drop to his ankles. Lorraine looked at him in disbelief as he climbed on top of her. She could feel him rubbing his limp dick up and down her vagina, trying to get himself hard. But Herman was so drunk, he couldn't get his soldier to stand at attention for nothing. He was so frustrated about it that he cocked back and smacked Lorraine again.

"You crazy bitch. Carry yo ass up those steps!" Herman demanded, getting up from the couch.

He stumbled backwards as he tried to pull his pants back up, damn near falling into the floor model TV in the middle of the living room.

Lorraine, who was just about naked, eased up slowly from the couch, holding her face. She did what she was told and walked up the stairs and then disappeared into their bedroom, leaving Herman to storm out of the house in a rage.

Jonathan cocked a bullet into the chamber of the AR-15, placed it on the table, and then picked up the 10mm and stuffed it with bullets. Kevin and A.J. stood around the table doing the same thing, loading and wiping down the guns they were about to use. Weed smoke clouded the dining room and the silence around the table indicated that all three men were focused on the task at hand.

A knock at the door took all three men out of their zone. Jonathan knew that it couldn't be Gator, she had just left thirty minutes ago to get her hair and nails done. He quickly slid the clip into the 10mm. He proceeded to open the door with the gun in his hand. When he looked out of the small window next to the entrance, Kasy was standing there looking back at him.

"Damn, my nigga, I didn't think that you was coming," Jonathan said when he opened the door.

Kasy had been falling back over the past few months, keeping his hands in the drug game to a minimum until he got through the couple of drug cases he had caught during the spring. When Jonathan told him he needed him to help out with a situation, and that a nice piece of money was involved, naturally, he jumped at the opportunity. Mainly because he was Brianna's little brother, and more than likely it wasn't anything serious.

When Kasy walked into the dining room and saw all of the guns out on the table, he glanced over at Jonathan with a surprised look on his face. It kind of caught him off guard to see Jonathan with all that heavy artillery.

"What the Fuck is y'all lil niggas about to do?" Kasy asked, looking around the room at A.J. and Kevin who were locked in and loading their weapons.

"We about to take something down, old head. I got a nice lick lined up right now," Jonathan told Kasy. "I could use an extra man on this one. That's why I called you."

Kasy stood there, shocked to hear this coming from Jonathan. It wasn't all that long ago that Jonathan graduated from high school and was supposed to be a college boy. This was a major step up in the street life for him, but from the looks of things, it seemed that he was all in. One thing Kasy hardly ever turned down was the chance to make some quick money, so it didn't take much convincing from Jonathan to get Kasy on board.

"Y'all lil niggas is crazy," Kasy said, picking up the blunt out of the ashtray. "Tell me what da lick read," he said, taking a pull of the weed.

Jonathan broke it down in the lowest degree on what was about to transpire. The homework that he did on this take down was perfected to the tee. He had precise timing and accurate locations of where he wanted to strike. Anyone who got in the way of what he was trying to accomplish during the lick were subject to be shot. This was the kind of work that was right up Kasy's alley. Jonathan even reminded Kasy of himself when he used to take down money getting niggas back in the day.

"Look, lil nigga. Ima ride wit you on dis one, but you better not say a word about this to ya sista," Kasy smiled, throwing a playful jab at Jonathan.

They all busted out laughing at the joke, but Kasy was the first one to stop laughing. "Nah lil nigga, I am serious about ya sister," Kasy said, looking around the room to make sure he had everyone's understanding on what he had just said.

"Yeah, I got you," Jonathan responded, nodding his head in agreement. "Now, let's get dis money, my nigga," he said, grabbing the Backwood from Kasy and taking a pull.

Lorraine stood in the bathroom mirror looking at the bruises on her face. The cut on her top lip looked like it needed stitches, but Lorraine wasn't about to be sitting up in the hospital looking stupid. Southern women were tough as nails, and most of the time, domestic disputes were handled in house. If a man put his hand on a woman from the south, he sure as hell better sleep with one eye open for a while. Lorraine didn't show it much, but Herman knew that she was a little crazy. That's why he hadn't been back in the house since he left a couple of hours ago.

"Who in the hell is that?" Lorraine mumbled, hearing the house phone ring.

She walked out of the bathroom and into her bedroom and grabbed the phone off her nightstand. "Hello!" she answered, looking out her bedroom window for any signs of Herman.

"Hey Mom," Brianna responded. "Is everything ok? You sound tense... I was just calling to see if you was coming today?"

"Coming where, baby?" Lorraine asked, patting the cut on her lip with a warm washrag.

"To court, you know the D.A. is going to cross examine Charrise today!"

Lorraine was silent. She had forgotten about the trial after the drama with Herman.

"Mom! Are you still there?" Brianna asked, noticing the dead silence.

"Yes, I am still here, baby. I don't think I am gonna make it today. I want to, but Herman was supposed to be taking me somewhere in a bit," Lorraine lied. "Just call and let me know how it goes." she suggested, looking into the mirror mounted on her dresser.

There was no way in hell Lorraine was going to let Brianna or any of her kids for that matter, see her face bruised the way it was. She knew that Herman would be as good as dead if they found out that he put his hands on their mother. Lorraine wasn't justifying Herman's attack, but she had to admit to herself that she was out of pocket for going to Cowboy's trial. At the end of the day, she was still married to Herman, and her loyalty was supposed to be with him.

"Alright then, Mom. I'll call you later when I get some time," Brianna said, before hanging up the phone.

Lorraine hung up the phone and then sat on the bed, trying to figure out how she was going to deal with Herman when he walked back through that door. She was still debating on whether or not to bust him upside his head with something for putting his hands on her the way he did, or just leave it alone and give him a pass on account that she was part of the problem that got it to that point. Whatever was going to happen would totally be up to Herman's actions when he came back home. If he walked through the door still on his bullshit, Lorraine was going to make sure her face wouldn't be the only face that was bruised up. But if he came in humble, sober, and apologetic, it was a good chance Lorraine was going to try to work things out. The choice was his, and if he knew what was best for him, he had better choose the latter instead of coming back home drunk.

Brianna, Charrise, Selena and Chatima all rushed into the courtroom just in time to hear the clerk yell, “All rise!” as the judge entered the courtroom.

Cowboy turned and looked back at them and then over at Casteno, who looked back with concern on his face. Today, Charrise was supposed to get back on the stand so that the D.A. could cross examine her about her testimony.

“Is the state ready to proceed?” the judge asked, lowering his glasses to the edge of his nose.

“Yes, Your Honor,” the D.A. answered and then looked over at Cowboy’s table. “Are we good?” he leaned over and asked Casteno.

Before he got a chance to answer, Charrise put her bag down on the bench right behind the defense table and walked up to the stand. She was sworn in by the clerk and then the D.A. went right at her like a lion on a zebra in the Sahara. He questioned her truthfulness about the whole kidnapping and whether or not she was really pregnant. He tried everything, hoping to get her to contradict herself or flat out lie.

Charrise did not bend or fold to the D.A.’s tactics. The hardest thing about trying to get somebody to lie, is trying to get somebody to lie when they’re actually telling the truth. It was easy for Charrise to do her thing and to crush any doubts about whether or not she was pregnant. She brought the abortion receipt to prove it. That really crushed the D.A., so much so that he became frustrated and decided to end the cross examination early before it got any worse.

"We'll have a short recess and then we can have the closing arguments from each side," the judge said before getting up and heading back to his chambers.

Casteno requested that Cowboy remain in the courtroom during the break, which was granted by one of the Sheriffs that he knew.

"Thanks Charrise, for everything," Cowboy began. "You really took a chance by taking the stand for me, and I want you to know that I am grateful for that, no matter what happens." Cowboy told Charrise with the most sincere look in his eyes.

"I guess that makes us even. You saved my life, and now hopefully, I saved yours," Charrise responded with a smile.

Once the recess was over, closing arguments lasted a little more than an hour. The D.A. tried to tell the jury not to believe Charrise's because it didn't make sense. He then went on about the evidence that was found at the scene of the crime, and how evidence proved that Cowboy had killed at least two of the three men in the house. At some point during the closing arguments, the jury looked like they had been persuaded by the D.A. and what he had presented, but then Casteno took the floor.

Casteno went off. He presented nothing but the facts that were established during the trial. One being the fact that Cowboy did kill two of the three men in the house, but the reason why he did it was in self-defense. Casteno used the testimony of Charrise who said that Cowboy found her from the address that the kidnappers gave him. He told the jury that once Cowboy got to the location where Charrise was at, he was fired upon first. He said that Cowboy returned fire only in self-defense. Casteno not only made it look like self-defense, but he also made Cowboy looked like a scared father trying to save his daughter.

By the end of the day, Cowboy looked like a hero instead of a murderer. It was getting late in the day, so the judge gave the jury the rest of the day off and postponed deliberations until Monday. That was crazy because everyone in the courtroom was hoping to get a quick verdict. Now, they would have to wait until after the weekend.

Jonathan and A.J. sat in the black Chevy Caprice with tinted windows waiting on the white Aston Martin to pull out of the Arlington Condominiums parking lot. Kevin was in a stolen burgundy Plymouth, already waiting inside the same parking lot, while Kasy had taken over the tollbooth at the entrance/exit point. Everyone was in position, locked, loaded, and ready to go.

"Look alive, y'all." Jonathan spoke through the walkie-talkie. "She should be coming out any second," he said, looking down at his watch.

Like clockwork, three black females got off the elevator and walked out onto the second level. Kevin could see that at least one of the women was armed as she rested her hand on the butt of her gun while looking around the badly lit parking lot. The other two women stood by the elevator door, while the one female scoured the parking lot for any danger.

Kevin sank as low as he possibly could in the driver seat, damn near to the point where he was on the floor. The armed female walked right past the car and didn't notice Kevin inside. Moments later, the same women walked back over to the elevator where she had a brief conversation with the other two females. For a minute, Kevin thought that he had been spotted. He sat back up in his seat and took the safety off both of his handguns.

"Alright girl, I will see you in a few hours," the main female said as she walked over to the Aston Martin.

One of the other females got into the car while the armed female stood and waited for the elevator. As the Aston Martin pulled out of its spot, Kevin started the engine to his car and then crept out of the parking space. He followed behind the car at an unnoticeable speed, watching as she pulled up to the tollbooth.

As soon as the car same to a stop, Kasy pulled the mask down over his face. The driver of the Aston Martin didn't even notice the masked man until she looked up from getting her parking pass out of the bag.

"Oh shit!" she yelled, seeing the ski masked bandit.

She threw the car in reverse, but slammed right into Kevin, who pushed her car forward. The driver reached into her bag, wrapped her hand around a 9mm Taurus, and then fired into the booth at Kasy.

Bullets crashed through the Aston Martin window and went right into the booth. Kasy got low to the ground and then kicked open the back door of the booth and began firing back at the car.

The loud roar from the .50 Cal rang out through the parking lot. Both females rolled out of the car, one shooting at Kasy while the other shot at Kevin.

It was an all-out shootout nearly at close range. Jonathan and A.J. pulled out of their parking spots and spun into the entrance of the parking garage. The female driver turned around and threw a few shots at the black Caprice, hitting the hood of it.

"Damn!" the female yelled out in the elevator as she heard the shots in the parking lot. "Come on, come on." she said, smacking the elevator button for the ground level.

Jonathan ducked the bullets that hit his windshield and hood of the car, and hopped out with the AR-15. He let it rip.

Both females jumped behind a parked car off to the side. The large assault rifle knocked holes the size of softballs in the car. The female driver popped out her clip to find that it only had one bullet left. The female passenger was all out too, but knew that if she could make it back to the car that she could grab another clip.

"I got one shot left," the female driver said, looking at the passenger.

She went to get up and let off her final shot, but ran right into the back of Kasy's gun. Craaack!

He hit her right across the top of her nose, knocking her to the ground. He quickly turned the gun on the female passenger. "Bitch, you better not move," Kasy threatened, pointing the gun directly in her face.

Kevin ran over to assist Kasy, grabbing a handful of the female passenger's hair, he lifted her to her feet. Kasy did the same thing, grabbing the female driver by the back of her collar and lifting her to her feet as well. They led both of the females to the back of the Caprice where Jonathan had the trunk already open.

The third female got off the elevator firing. Jonathan lifted the large AR-15 waist high and let off about ten shots in her direction. She ran behind a parked car trying to get out of the way of the hot balls.

"That'll hold her." Jonathan said, opening the driver side door and jumping out of the car.

Kasy slammed the trunk of the car on the two females, but when he was about to get into the backseat, he looked over and saw Kevin lying on the ground.

A.J. noticed it too, jumped out of the car, and ran over to him. Jonathan looked from the driver side.

The third female had gotten off a better shot than she'd thought. One of the bullets hit Kevin in the side of his head, killing him instantly.

The female jumped up from behind the car and let off several more shots. Kasy returned fire, forcing her to duck back behind the car.

"Come on!" he yelled out to A.J., who was standing over Kevin like he didn't want to leave him.

The sounds of sirens blared in the far distance. Kasy knew that he did not have a lot of time before the cops got there. He grabbed A.J. by his arm and pulled him into the car. Jonathan slammed the gear in reverse and sped out the parking lot onto the street.

The female let off a few more shots as the Caprice pulled off down the street. She walked over to Kevin, stood over top of his body, and let her last shot off into his head.

"Yo cuz, you might spank dis shit." Cowboy's celly, Booda, said, standing over the sink washing out a t-shirt. "If homegirl did dat for you, it ain't no way the jury gone find you guilty."

"Yeah youngblood, it looks good, but one thing I know about these people is that it's never over until they say not guilty. Ya dig?"

"Yeah, well just send a nigga some flicks when you get home." Booda chuckled wringing the water out of his t-shirt.

A few minutes went by and then the unit correctional officer walked up to the cell door and tapped on it with her flashlight. "Cowboy, you got a visit," she said sliding the visiting pass to him under his door.

Cowboy knew that it had to be Brianna coming to see him. She had been riding so hard for him ever since she found out that he was her dad, and Cowboy was loving every minute of it. The more they talked, the closer they became. It was almost as if he didn't miss 27 years of her life. Yeah, his baby girl was definitely his child. She was sweet like her mother, but if pushed, she would take your ass out without a second thought. He hated missing so much of her life, but he would do what he could to make up for lost time.

“Boy, you stay getting visits,” Dennison, one of the guards who knew Cowboy said when he walked up to the visiting room door.

Cowboy nodded to Dennison who opened the door to the booth. Cowboy sat down in the small metal chair in front of the thick fiberglass window. He watched the other inmates speaking to their families and lawyers. The door opened on the other side and Herman smiled at him. He took a seat and picked up the receiver. Cowboy got up and knocked on the door for the CO. He wasn’t about to entertain this weak ass fool.

Herman tapped on the window. “What, you can’t give the man that raised your bastard child a few minutes?” he yelled. “Yeah, you ain’t no man. Look at you, running away again.”

Cowboy sighed. This dude was making his fuckin skin crawl and his blood boil. He turned and walked back to the glass and reluctantly picked up the receiver.

“I am not gonna take up too much of your time, big man. I was just hoping that we can talk, man to man.” Herman said, smirking at Cowboy.

“Man to man?” Cowboy asked, gritting his teeth. “You consider yourself to be a man? Aren’t you the same dumb fool that agreed to have your own daughter kidnapped, and almost got her murdered?" Cowboy said, clenching the receiver.

"Oh, and you daddy of the fucking century, huh? You have sex with a married woman, get her pregnant, and then leave your bastard for another to take care of? I raised your child like she was my own. Took care of her and her hoeing ass mama, busting my ass working 12 to 16 hours a damn day six days a fucking week to provide for them. I know what being a father is about, nigga!" Herman shot back.

"Yeah, Brianna told me about how much you *provided* for her. Making her feel like an outsider, emotionally beating her and Lorraine down. Yeah, you like the fucking system, giving her a roof over her head, and food. Thanks for doing that, but don't say you raised her as one of your own. We both know that ain't true. If it were, you wouldn't have sold her out so easily to have her killed." Cowboy said.

"I don't and never have given a fuck about that little bitch. You right… I hate yo ass and I hate her. As far as I am concerned, the moment she took her first breath should have also been her last. I had to take care of her ass because my wife went through with the pregnancy, and I had a reputation. That is the only reason I didn't smother her ass at night."

Cowboy wanted to jump through the glass and beat Herman to death with his bare hands. "You know that I'm gonna kill you when I get out of here," Cowboy said, clutching the receiver tighter.

"Oh, and about that. I don't think that you will be getting out of here no time soon. I know my little girl testified on your behalf the other day," he said, referring to Charrise taking the stand. "You might beat the triple homicide, but you can't escape killing Tank in my house. Ya dumb ass daughter was stupid enough to bury the body in my backyard, but guess where I moved it to? I buried him in your backyard, and guess who is holding onto the murder weapon? Yep, your daughter. I'ma kill both of you at the same time," Herman taunted with a devious grin on his face.

Cowboy's vision became blurry and he felt his head begin to swim. He threw the phone receiver at the glass, picked up the chair and began hitting the glass with it. Two guards rushed into the room and grabbed him. Cowboy slung them off him, and smashed the chair against the glass one more time, sending it shattering towards Herman. He jumped through the opening, and lunged at Herman. Cowboy's right hook knocked Herman to the floor. He slammed Herman's head against the concrete flooring.

Something burned his back, and his body froze. He heard the zapping sound of the taser. A guard ran to Herman, who was stretched out on the floor, as four other guards placed restraints on Cowboy. The other visitors watched as Cowboy was taken out of the area by the guards, and the guards helped Herman to his feet.

"He tried to kill me!" Herman whined as he sat in the chair holding his jaw and the back of his head.

Cowboy was immediately escorted out of the visiting area, and the only thing he could think about was getting back to the unit to call Brianna.

To say that Jonathan and his crew had done their homework on these women, was an understatement. They pulled into the small office complex that they had followed the women to on many occasions. They still had both of the women they had snatched from the parking lot in the trunk. Inside the car was silent as all three men thought about their fallen soldier. Kasy, being the veteran of the group, let them know that he understood their pain and knew it was a tough pill to swallow. But right now wasn't the time for mourning. The completion of the mission at hand was top priority. If anything went wrong now, Kevin's death would have been in vain.

"You right, big brah. Yo, help me get dese bitches out the back," Jonathan said as he exited the car, putting a mask over his face.

Kasy and A.J. followed suit and placed their masks over their faces as well. Both got out of the car with Jonathan and walked to the back of the vehicle. Jonathan looked around the parking lot before pulling the chrome .380 from his back pocket. The coast was clear, so Jonathan nodded for Kasy to open the trunk, and when he did both of the women looked up at the men with anger in their faces. The ladies were pulled out and thrown to the ground.

The female driver of the Aston Martin looked around the familiar surroundings in disbelief. She looked up at the masked men and wondered who they were.

"Y'all must don't know who y'all fuckin wit." the female said, brushing the dirt off of her pants.

"Bitch, shut up!" Jonathan shot back, grabbing her by the hair and pulling her to her feet. "Now, get ya mafuckin ass ova there before I put a bullet in ya head," he threatened, pushing her in the back.

At gunpoint, the three men led the two girls a short distance inside the building until they came to a warehouse door with a sign on it that read, "Elite Delivery Company." Jonathan reached into the pocket of one of the women and grabbed some keys. He had watched them do it so many times that he picked the right key on the first try. He pushed the door open and then pushed the girls inside. At this point, the female driver knew what it was.

Jonathan had sat on her day and night and watched how she came to this location at least twice a week with a large duffle bag. Every time the female left the building, the bag always seemed to look a little lighter than it was when she first went in with it. That is how Jonathan knew this had to be the stash spot. It was a good stash spot too, because even when he attempted to search the building later, he couldn't find anything. He and Gator had even tried together, with no success.

"Now, I know it's in here," Jonathan began. "You got two choices. You can either give me what you got hidden here or you can make this your final resting place."

She looked up at them. "It's nothing in here," the female lied, hoping that the masked men would believe her.

A.J. pulled the black .45 automatic out of his waist and placed it on the back of her head. The female could feel it pressed up against the rear of her skull, and for a second she thought she was dead. She looked over at the other girl, trying not to be the first one to break. If she was going to die, she didn't want it to be like this. Money was something that could be replaced.

"How do I know that after I give you what you want, you won't kill us once you got it?" the female asked, trying to get a feel for whether or she was going to die or make it out alive.

"If I was gonna kill you, I wouldn't have a mask on right now." Jonathan responded.

She slowly walked over to the plaque hanging on the wall, lifted the twenty-pound plate and set it on the ground. Jonathan smiled under the mask at the sight of the large safe underneath. The female began to turn the dial on the safe, but Jonathan quickly snapped out of his zone and stopped her.

"Back up from the safe," he told the female, pointing the gun at her. He didn't have any idea what was inside, and he wasn't going to take the chance of her opening the safe and reaching in to grab a gun. Gator had schooled him that most people kept a pistol where they stashed their money. It was sort of a hustler's code, and it was a good thing that Jonathan thought about it, because after the female gave him the combination to the safe and he cracked it open, the very first thing that sat at the front of the door was a gun.

He looked at the female and shook his head. The safe was pretty big. It was about four feet in length and about three feet high. There was so much money packed inside the safe that Jonathan had trouble pulling it out. It took every bit of ten minutes for him to clear the safe completely, placing all the money on top of a large warehouse table. He sent Kasy back out to the car for more bags to put the rest of the money in and he was back within minutes.

"Well, look shawty, I got some good news and some bad news," Jonathan said as he watched Kasy take the last of the money out of the building.

The female just shook her head, knowing that she should not have trusted him. "I gave you my word that I wasn't going to kill you, and I'ma stand by that. But unfortunately, your friend gotta die," Jonathan said. He pointed his gun at the other female and pulling the trigger.

The close range shot to the center of her forehead almost lifted her off her feet. Her body rocked back and then fell face first into the dusty floor.

"I think a life for a life is fair. Y'all killed my boy, so..." Jonathan said, shrugging.

The female sat there and stared at her friend's lifeless body on the ground. She began to weep for her fallen friend, but secretly was glad that she had escaped the same fate. The woman was so wrapped up in thanking God for sparing her life that she didn't even notice the men leave.

Herman slammed the shovel into the dirt and dug as fast as he could, periodically looking over his shoulders to see if any of his neighbors were watching him. He knew that he didn't have too much time to get the body dug up and out of his backyard before Brianna was clear down his throat. He wished that he hadn't lied to Cowboy about already digging up Tank's corpse, but anger along with the satisfaction of seeing the look on Cowboy's face when he told him seemed worth it.

"What in the hell is that man doing?" Lorraine mumbled to herself, looking into the backyard from the kitchen.

She had no idea that Brianna had a body buried in their backyard, and for a scary moment, Lorraine thought that Herman was digging the hole for her. Ever since he came home yesterday, they hadn't said a single word to each other, but he seemed to be in a better mood. Herman stopped digging, turned and looked around the yard. He couldn't seem to figure out where the body was buried. He only dug in that particular spot because that was where the fountains weere placed, but from the looks of the empty four foot hole that he dug, the body wasn't there.

"Come on," Herman said to himself, scratching his head, "Where the hell is it?"

He looked around the yard again and saw another patch of grass that looked shady, about 20 yards out. He walked over and began digging. The sun was heavily beaming down on his head, causing him to sweat profusely, but even still, he continued to dig. The more he dug, the more a foul stench began to seep through the ground.

"God damn!" he yelled after his shovel jammed into, what he believed to be the chest of the rotting corpse.

He looked around again to see if anybody was watching him. The smell from the body stunk, so badly that Herman had to put some more dirt over it until he was ready to move it. Lorraine was almost tempted to go outside and see what he was up to, but decided against it to avoid starting an argument. One thing she did do was keep a sharp eye out on him. She had an old .38 special, readily available for her to protect herself in the event that one of those holes he had dug was indeed for her.

A.J. and Jonathan pulled up to Kevin's house. The news of his death was on every local evening newscast. Both boys knew they had to show their faces soon and make sure that Kevin's family was straight. It was a crowd of people standing in front of the small duplex. Mainly because it was no way all of them could fit in the tiny house. Only family was allowed inside at the moment. The only close friends that Kevin had truly ever acknowledged were Jonathan and A.J. They had been rolling with each other since the 2nd grade, day for day. A.J. and Jonathan were considered to be more family than most of the people that were there.

"Damn man, I can't go in there. I know Ms. Matty is in there," A.J. said, stopping at the front steps.

Ms. Matty was Kevin's Mom. She like both of their mothers had watched all of the boys grow up together. A.J. knew that she was going to want some answers that he wasn't strong enough to tell her. She was like a second mom to both him and Jonathan, and the one thing that he was never capable of doing was lying to her. He would rather not say anything, then to try to lie and get caught by her.

"I got you, brah, but we got to show our faces. Let me handle it… you just wait out here." Jonathan said, getting out the car and starting to walk up the stairs and into the house.

The moment he walked through the door, he could hear the cries of Kim, Kevin's sister. When he walked into the living room area, there she was, balled up on the couch crying her eyes out. Kim's girlfriend sat beside her, trying her best to comfort her. Jonathan didn't even know where to begin or who to begin with, because as he turned his head away from Kim, he made eye contact with Ms. Matty who was sitting at the kitchen table smoking a cigarette. Jonathan's eyes began to water. He knew he was in trouble, because she seemed to be calm.

Ms. Matty took another pull of the Newport and then tossed it into the ashtray before waving at Jonathan. She motioned for him to come back to the kitchen with her. His feet instantly felt like cinderblocks as he slowly made his way down the short hallway that seemed like it was the length of a mile.

"Come on in here, boy," Ms. Matty said, pulling the extra chair out from under the table.

"Hi Ms. Matty," Jonathan said, leaning in and giving her a kiss on the cheek, while wiping the tears from his face.

She sat there with a relaxed look. There were no signs of her crying, nor did she seem bitter about the death of Kevin, which was odd, considering that he was her only boy. "How's Lorraine?" she asked, grabbing one of Jonathan's hands and placing them both between hers. He wanted to snatch his hands back because it seem like her touch was pushing all of her silent pain into his body, and he felt like he would break down at any moment. He took a deep sigh and managed to get out a few words.

"She's good, more than likely she will be over here sometime today."

"Yeah, yeah, that's good, Jonathan," she said with a smile. "You know babe, I wanna ask you something, and I know that you're gonna tell me the truth because you are a good boy." Ms. Matty continued.

Jonathan could see where this was going, and he knew that the question that the next question was about to be major. "You know, you and my son are like brothers. Right along with that A.J. who I seen sitting out in the car, and I'm guessing he can't muster up the strength to come in here and face me." she said, looking back outside and seeing A.J. standing at the bottom of the steps. "Y'all boys were so close. If he used the bathroom, you would pass him the toilet paper to wipe his ass and A.J. would flush the toilet." She chuckled. The sound of her laughter didn't match the emotion that was starting to show on her face.

Jonathan could see how she was setting up the foundation for her question. She was boxing him into a corner where anything less than the truth would sound stupid. There wouldn't be any way possible for him not to know the answer to her question. He knew he couldn't sit there and lie to her face about what had happened to her Kevin.

"Baby, please tell me what happened to my son?" she asked, looking Jonathan directly in his eyes.

Jonathan sat there stuck. He knew that she was building up to this question, and yet he still wasn't prepared to answer it. This was harder than he thought it would be, and as he looked into her eyes, he could now see how A.J. felt about lying to her.

When Jonathan walked out of Kevin's house, A.J. could see that the conversation he had with the family did not go too well. As Jonathan came storming down the steps A.J. could see the stains on his face where tears once flowed. This was the first time in all of the years A.J. had known Jonathan that he saw him cry.

"Yo, what happened?" He asked, walking behind Jonathan on his way back to the car.

Jonathan didn't answer him right away. He was still upset about what had just gone on. It was the hardest thing he ever had to do in his life.

"Yo, what did you tell her?" A.J. asked again as he stood by the passenger side of the car.

Jonathan stood by the driver side looking over at A.J. "I told her the truth, my nigga…" he said, looking over at Kevin's house. "She deserved to know what happened, and I know that our brother would have wanted me to tell her." Jonathan said, before opening his door and getting in the car.

"What did she say?" A.J. asked, getting into the car behind him. "You think she is gonna go to the cops?"

"Nah, she's not gonna go to the cops. Ms. Matty loves us too much for that. She said that we're gonna have to live with Kevin's death for the rest of our lives. She said that alone was going to be enough punishment for our actions." Jonathan told A.J.

Ms. Matty was 100% right, because Jonathan was already feeling the devastating effects of Kevin's death. He had to carry the weight of that responsibility the most, because the whole idea was his in the first place. If it wasn't for him, Kevin would still be alive, and that was the thing that ate away at him.

Charrise sat in the passenger side quiet, just listening to Brianna spaz out on the phone with who she assumed was Auntie.

"What you mean, she trying to come direct? I'm the one who brought her to you, now you telling me the bitch trying to cut a side deal?" Brianna yelled as she held her phone in her left hand and picked up Charrise's to call Selena.

"Lena, you know your bitch, Gwen, trying to cut a side deal on us with Auntie?" Brianna asked.

"Bri, are you serious? I know she wouldn't do something like that, especially how we looked out for her with her son situation and everything. It must be some type of misunderstanding."

"Yeah that's what I was thinking, but I got Auntie on the other line and that's what she saying. What I need you to do is setup a meeting with her so we can get this shit straightened out ASAP."

"Got it Bri, I'll hit you back with when and where... one."

Charrise didn't want to admit it, but she kind of liked Gwen. She liked the boss like attitude she had, along with the way she carried herself. Granted, if she would have even thought about making a move on Brianna, Charrise wouldn't hesitate to put a bullet in her head.

Brianna hung up with Auntie as she pulled into Lorraine's driveway. Charrise had a disturbed look on her face. Brianna looked over, and by the time she realized what she had done, Charrise was already in tears. She hadn't been to her mother's house since the day she was kidnapped right in front of the same house. The only time she saw her mother and father was when they were somewhere else.

"Damn, I'm sorry, sis." Brianna said, covering her face with both of her hands. "Come on, let's get out of here," Brianna suggested.

"No, no, no, it's cool. I think I needed this." Charrise responded, wiping the tears from her face.

"I haven't seen Mommy in a few days anyway," she said, opening the door.

They knocked on the door but there wasn't any answer. Brianna looked around for Herman's car which wasn't anywhere in sight. They were about to leave when Charrise remembered that she still had the keys to the house. She reached into her Michael Kors bag and retrieved them. She unlocked both locks and then opened the door.

"Mom! Dad!" Charrise yelled, entering the house.

Lorraine sat upstairs in her bedroom looking out the window at the two empty holes in the backyard. The sound of Charrise yelling her name startled her a little. She didn't know if her ears were deceiving her, because for the past few months, Charrise had refused to step foot in the house. Lorraine began to walk out of the bedroom to go to her, but stopped when she passed by the mirror and saw that her face was still bruised pretty good from Herman's attack.

"Mom!" Charrise yelled out again, walking up the steps.

Brianna stayed downstairs to look for Lorraine in the kitchen. Lorraine looked around the room in a panic, trying to decide whether or she should hide from Charrise, but as soon as she moved towards the closet, Charrise opened the bedroom door. Lorraine had made it to the closet and had the door open when Charrise walked in. She played it like she was looking for something.

"Mom, I know you heard me calling you. What are you doing up here?" she asked, walking up behind her mother.

When Lorraine turned around, the smile that Charrise had on her face turned into a frown instantly. Not only were the bruises visible, but they were also fresh. The first person that came to mind was Herman.

"He put his hands on you?" Charrise asked, reaching up and lightly touching the side of her face.

Lorraine put her head down, ashamed that her daughter had to see her like this.

"Brianna!" Charrise yelled out. "Brianna, get up here!" she continued yelling.

When Brianna didn't answer nor come up the steps, Charrise grabbed Lorraine by the arm and pulled her out of the room and down the stairs. Brianna hadn't answered because she was stuck, staring out of the kitchen window at the two holes that Herman had dug up. She didn't have to go outside to see that Tank's body was missing from his grave.

"Bri, look at dis shit." Charrise said, walking into the kitchen with Lorraine behind her. Brianna turned around from the window to see her mother's battered face. She was furious.

"Who did dis shit to you? Was it Herman?" Brianna yelled, unable to control her anger.

Lorraine took a seat at the kitchen table and began to tell the story of how Herman was in the courtroom the day that she attended Cowboy's trial. She even made excuses for him, saying that she didn't have any business supporting Cowboy when she was a married woman. Brianna wasn't trying to hear none of that. She didn't care what the circumstances were; Herman did not have to put his hands on her mother.

"Where did he go?" Brianna asked, turning around and looking out the kitchen window at the empty grave.

"I don't know where he went. He did whatever he did in the backyard and then left out of here," Lorraine answered.

Charrise walked over to the window and looked out into the backyard. She didn't have the slightest idea that Tank was buried back there, nor did she know the story behind why. It wasn't even that important to her at the moment. All she wanted to do was find Herman and check him about hitting her mother. Brianna wanted to do the same thing in finding Herman, but just not for the same reasons. It was something more important at stake right now. If Herman knew what to do with the body he had just discovered, it could easily get ugly for Brianna and whoever else he felt like screwing around.

Cowboy paced back and forth in his cell waiting for the lieutenant to come down the range. Right after the visit with Herman, Cowboy was taken straight to the hole, courtesy of Herman telling the Captain on his way out the door that Cowboy threatened to have him and his family killed. The Captain reacted swiftly by sending Cowboy to the hole for the rest of the weekend until he sorted everything out.

"C/O!" Cowboy yelled as he kicked the cell door. "C/O!" he continued, kicking the door and pushing the panic button.

The panic button was something that the guards could not ignore. It was policy that they had to check on the inmate, in case a medical emergency had occurred. The guard took his time coming down the range, seeing that it was Cowboy.

"Mr. Parsons, you better have a medical emergency," the guard said walking up to the door.

"Yo, I told you to get the LT down here. It's an emergency," Cowboy yelled back, looking through the thin glass. "You said the Lt. was coming down here, and he ain't come through yet."

"I told you, Mr. Parsons, he is making his rounds. As a matter of fact, he is doing it as we speak," the guard told Cowboy.

Ironically, the Lt. walked on the range just as the guard was going back to the bubble. He looked into every cell that he passed, and when he got up to Cowboy's door, he was standing there waiting.

"Lt., why you got me in the hole? I didn't do shit." Cowboy said.

"You're under the Captain's review. Word is you should be getting out on Monday." Lt. explained.

Monday was almost two days away, and Cowboy needed to contact Brianna now in order to warn her about Herman. Normally, Brianna would come to see Cowboy on the weekend, but when she did not come up, Cowboy had a feeling that something was wrong.

"Look Lt... I wouldn't be asking you this if it wasn't an emergency. I really need to call my daughter. I haven't used the phone since I been down here. Can you please let me come out to at least make a phone call?" Cowboy pleaded in a low and respectful voice.

The Lt. looked at Cowboy and could see the concern written all over his face. Actually, a phone call was something easy the Lt. could sign off on, and in this case, he did just that.

"I will get the guard to let you out for 15 minutes when I leave off of this range. Do what you need to do and don't cause any problems." he said before walking off to finish making his rounds.

As promised, as soon as the Lt. walked off the range, Cowboy's door was opened and he was allowed to come out. He tried to call Brianna's phone, but it kept going straight to voicemail. He tried the whole 15 minutes he was out, but still got no answer. That didn't do anything but make him more worried than he was before. Stressed out to the max, all Cowboy could do was head back to his cell and pray that God watched over his little girl.

The inside of Brianna's car was dead silent the whole ride back to her house. The sisters had convinced Lorraine to come stay with them for a while, or at least until Brianna and Charrise had the opportunity to confront Herman about the situation. Nobody knew how long that could take, since he was missing in action.

Herman couldn't be found anywhere. They drove around and checked his favorite drinking spots, along with the local eateries he liked. Still, there was no Herman. Getting Lorraine back to her place was all Brianna could do for now. Eventually, he would surface again, and when he did, Brianna was going to do what she should have done a long time ago, which was put Herman in his final resting place.

Chapter 10

Monday morning came fast, and by noon, the call came in that the jury had reached a verdict. Court was set for 2:00pm. Lorraine declined going to the courthouse with Brianna and Charrise out of fear that Herman would be there. Instead, Selena accompanied her back to her house so she could grab a few things she needed. When they pulled up to the house, Herman's car was in the driveway. Lorraine was a little reluctant at first to go into the house, but Selena made her feel a lot more comfortable when she reached under the driver seat and pulled a large caliber handgun out, and placed it on her lap.

"Don't worry about anything. Just get what you need and we're out of here." Selena said, cocking a bullet into the chamber.

"Herman!" Lorraine called out once they entered the house. "Herman!" she yelled again, walking towards the stairs.

Herman wasn't answering, but Selena wasn't taking any chances. She followed Lorraine up the steps. Selena was given strict instructions from Brianna to shoot and kill Herman at any sign of aggression, and she wasn't going to hesitate for a second, especially if he jumped out of one of those rooms like he was crazy.

"I don't think he is here," Lorraine said, walking into her bedroom. "He would have made himself noticed by now."

"Alright Mrs. Lorraine, the quicker you get ya things, the quicker we can get out of here." Selena said, looking down the hallway for any suspicious movement.

Lorraine went right to work, grabbing a trash bag from out her closet and filling it up with all the items she needed. Within ten minutes, she and Selena were loaded and heading out the door.

Jonathan, A.J., and Kasy sat at the table in Jonathan's dining room with a large mountain of money in front of them. This was the first time that any of the men had seen the proceeds from the lick. From the way that nobody really wanted to touch the blood money, it was obvious that this was a bittersweet moment.

"Yo, let's count dis shit up." Jonathan said, reaching over and grabbing a stack of money from the pile. "Kev's cut goes to his family. I'll take it over there later on." he said.

Both Kasy and A.J. nodded their heads in agreement. It was only right that his money be given to his family, and Jonathan wasn't going to see it no other way. He had really stepped up and become the heart of this crew. Even though Kasy was older and more experienced, he respected Jonathan's leadership skills, and what he had put together.

It took over four and a half hours for them to count up the 5, 10, 20, and 100 dollar bills. There wasn't a doubt in anybody's mind that this was dope money. At the end, it came out to 1.2 million, broken down four ways evenly. Everybody came out with a nice 300K. The leftover change was put to the side to pay for Kevin's funeral.

Brianna pulled up to the courthouse, not knowing what was going to happen. From the evidence that was presented to the jury, one would think that a not guilty verdict was the right thing to do. However, when the majority of the jury was older, white, suburban people, anything was liable to happen.

"Everything is gonna be alright," Charrise looked over and told Brianna after she finished parking.

Brianna had something else on her mind other than the trial. She was sitting there debating whether to tell Charrise that Herman was the one who set her up to be kidnapped. She didn't know how her sister was going to react to it, but at the same time, it was killing Brianna not to confide in her.

"I need to talk to you about something." Brianna said, turning to face Charrise.

"Sure, what's going on, Bri, and why the long face?" Charrise asked.

Brianna took in a deep breath. "Please don't be mad at me..." she said, shaking her head. "I'm not sure how to tell you this, other than to just say it. Herman was involved with you being kidnapped. Hakeem paid him to have you taken in order to draw me out. I was—"

"Wait, wait, what did you just say?" Charrise asked, snapping her head back with a twisted look on her face. "I know you didn't' just say that my dad was responsible for me being kidnapped," Charrise snapped.

"I know, I'm sorry," Brianna tried to plead, seeing how mad it had made Charrise.

The look she gave Brianna cut through her like a single edge razor. "You supposed to be my fucking sister and you hide some shit like this from me? You let this nigga walk around here day after day like he was my fuckin dad, holding me and comforting me!" Charrise yelled.

Brianna sat there in silence. There was nothing that she could say to make it better, nor was Charrise trying to hear anything. "You know what, Bri, it's cool. I guess you weren't my sister after all..." Charrise said, reaching into the backseat to get her Milly bag. "Dis shit between me and you is done. And don't fuckin follow me!" Charrise said, opening the door and getting out of the car.

As bad as Brianna wanted to get out of the car and chase her down, she didn't, knowing that Charrise needed her space right now. Bothering her would only make it worse. Brianna just sat there in the automobile and cried. She hoped that she didn't lose her sister and best friend.

After twenty minutes of trying to decide if she had done the right thing in telling Charrise about Herman's involvement, Brianna wiped the tears from her face and headed into the courthouse. Before she could sit down, Cowboy motioned for her to come to him.

"We got a problem, baby girl. Herman came to see me and he dug up that hidden treasure of ours." Cowboy whispered in her ear.

"I already know, Dad, and I'm working on it, but I have a couple of other issues as well right now."

Cowboy could see that she was in a daze. The whole courtroom was quiet as they waited for the jury to be brought in. Cowboy could not help but to notice that the stress in his daughter's eyes was not only because of the body that Herman had.

"What else is wrong?" he asked, reaching back and tapping her on the arm.

Brianna snapped out of her daze and quickly tried to put a smile on her face, but Cowboy wasn't going for that. He knew that it was something more. "Come on, spit it out," he said, trying to get her eyes to meet his. "If it has anything to do with the ..."

"Charrise knows about Herman," Brianna said, cutting him off. "I told her and she snapped on me," she said, shaking her head.

"Damn!" Cowboy exhaled, leaning back in his chair. "I knew dat shit was gonna come back and bite us in the ass. Does she know about the body?" he asked, referring to him killing Tank and burying him in Herman's backyard.

"She didn't even give me a chance to get to that. She jumped out of my car and told me not to follow her." Brianna said as she began to tear up.

"All rise!" the clerk announced before the judge entered the courtroom.

Cowboy and Brianna quickly halted their conversation. This was the moment that everyone had been waiting for. Someone walked out into the hallway and made the announcement that a verdict had been reached. People poured back into the courtroom. For the first time in history, Cowboy had butterflies in his stomach. If he were standing up, he probably would have buckled at the knees.

"Ok, it seems that the jury has reached a verdict. Please let them in." the judge said, taking his glasses off.

As the jury walked into the courtroom, all eyes were on them. The butterflies in Cowboy's stomach had found their way into Brianna's stomach as well. While all the others sat down, the foreman remained standing.

"I understand that you've reached a verdict," the judge said.

"Yes, Your Honor… unanimously." the foreman responded.

The judge looked down at the paper with the list of charges on it and began to read.

"In the charge of murder in the first degree, in count one of the indictment, for the murder of Hakeem Wilbourn, how does the jury find the defendant?" the judge asked, looking back up at the foreman.

"The jury finds the defendant ... Not guilty!" the foreman announced.

As the judge continued to read down the charges and ask for the verdicts, the foreman continued to say not guilty to the very end. The mixture of emotions from both Cowboy's supporters and the family of the victims filled the courtroom. It got so loud that the judge had to call for order.

Casteno leaned over and shook Cowboy's hand to congratulate him. The feeling that Cowboy had was beyond anything he had ever experienced before, and the only thing he could do was smile. Brianna couldn't stop smiling either as she leaned over and hugged her dad.

"We won!" Brianna joyfully proclaimed, trying her best to hold back the few tears that forced their way out of her eyes.

"Yeah, we did it, baby girl," Cowboy responded, satisfied with the results.

Jonathan sat on the front steps of St. Matthews Church listening to the many cries coming from inside the building. He took another swig of the orange soda bottle that was spiked with Ciroc and then looked out into the street where cars drove by, unaware that a real nigga was having his wake right now.

"Damn Kev... Why now?" Jonathan mumbled to himself, rubbing the top of his head.

Flashbacks of the time when Kevin took a puff of a cigarette for the first time brought Jonathan to laughter. He remembered Kevin choking for about ten minutes straight. Then he thought about the time when he, Kevin, and A.J. got drunk off a 40oz of Old English 800 they had convinced a junkie to purchase for them. Kevin threw up on A.J.'s brand new pair of Jordans, but only ruining the right shoe. A.J. still rocked the mismatched sneakers for a month before his mom bought him another pair.

Jonathan went from laughing to crying within seconds. As he sobbed, he felt a hand on his shoulder. When he looked up to see who it was, he put his head back down in shame.

"Ya friend would like to see you one last time, Jonathan," Ms. Matty said, pulling some tissue out of her pocket.

"Damn, Ms. Matty, I fucked up..." Jonathan cried, putting his face in his hands. "Dat should be me in there. He should be out here," he continued, letting the tears pour out of his eyes.

"Come on inside, Jonathan." Ms. Matty said, rubbing his back.

"I can't, Ms. Matty. I can't look at him like this."

"Jonathan! Now if you say that you love my son, you're gonna get up, wipe those tears from your face, and go in there and pay your respects to ya best friend." Ms. Matty demanded, and she wasn't taking no for an answer.

Jonathan could not believe it. After everything that had happened, Ms. Matty was still showing him love. Her son was lying in a coffin, partially because of him. And instead of shunning Jonathan, she did the total opposite. She helped Jonathan to his feet, wrapped him in her arms, and hugged him tight.

"I'm sorry." Jonathan cried, resting his head on her shoulder.

"I don't blame you, Jonathan. That could have easily been you, and I would want Lorraine to be doing the same thing that I'm doing right now." she said, wiping the few tears from his cheeks.

"Now let's go inside and see my boy." She smiled, leading him into the church.

Charrise pulled up to the front of the church. She and Lorraine got out so that they could pay their last respects. Brianna pulled in right behind them, also coming to show her respect. By the time they had gotten in there, the line to view the body was kind of short. Lorraine walked up, kissed Kevin on his head, and then walked over and gave Ms. Matty a hug and a kiss on the cheek. Jonathan was sitting right next to Ms. Matty, so Lorraine gave him the same thing. They were all like family. Growing up, Lorraine used to watch Kevin on the days Ms.Matty had the night shift at the hospital. Likewise, Ms. Matty used to watch Jonathan after he got out of school until Lorraine got home from work. That's just how close the two were, so naturally, the death of Kevin was a devastating blow for everyone.

Brianna was hoping that she and Charrise could have a conversation. However, she could tell that Charrise wasn't open for it, and today wasn't the time or place to push the issue.

"Did you see anybody familiar?" Gwen asked Crystal and Ivory as they walked up and took a seat on the park bench right next to her.

"No, not really. But I did see …" Crystal paused, not really sure what she saw was worth mentioning.

At that point, any and all information was useful in Gwen's eyes. She couldn't figure out for the love of God who was responsible for robbing her. Not only was she robbed, another MHB crew member was murdered, execution style. The sense of urgency to track down the culprits behind it was felt throughout the whole crew. Gwen took immediate action, first by finding out the identity of the male body that was left behind after the shootout. After finding out that it was Kevin Miles, she sent Crystal and Ivory to the funeral to scope things out.

"There was this one guy who stayed outside for most of the funeral."

"Then, this lady came outside and he began crying. I don't know what was said, because we were sitting in the car at the time." Ivory chimed in.

"Yeah, and when he did go into the church, he was sitting in the front row," Crystal said.

"Hell, which could be anybody." Gwen shot back, waving them off. "Is that all?"

"Oh, oh, and it was another guy that stood by the casket crying damn near the whole funeral." Ivory remembered.

Gwen sat there and thought about it for a minute. The actions of those two men showed that they had a lot of love for the deceased. They had to have either been family members or close friends, and Gwen was willing to bet that they were friends. And if they were close friends, then nine times out of ten they knew something, or maybe even were involved in some kind of way.

"Did you get these guys names?" Gwen asked, hoping that they did.

"No, we didn't get the names, but Ivory did write down a couple license plate numbers." Crystal advised.

"Yeah, and I think that I did get one of theirs." Ivory said, rambling through her back pocket for the piece of paper that she was writing on. "Oh, here it go."

She passed the folded up piece of paper to Gwen who looked down at the five license plate numbers. This piece of information was more valuable than Crystal thought. Gwen was definitely going to pursue the two cry babies who performed at the funeral. Before the week was out, she was gonna make it her business to find out just how much love the two men had for their dead comrade.

Brianna ran to Cowboy as he walked out of the jail. He picked her up and swung her around like she was a child, and she felt loved and protected.

"Daddy!" she said like a toddler as he carried her towards the awaiting Audi truck.

Brandon smiled as Cowboy placed Brianna back on the ground.

Cowboy extended his hand. "You must be Brandon..." He said as he shook Brandon's hand. "My little girl seems to be quite fond of you."

Brianna blushed at the sound of her father calling her his little girl. Hearing him say those words gave her something she had waited her entire life to feel: love from a man who would protect and love her unconditionally.

"I'm fond of her too, sir." Brandon said pulling Brianna close to him.

Cowboy nodded.

Brianna smirked as Cowboy's usual steely gaze fell on Brandon. After a few moments of silence, he smiled, and nodded. "So baby girl, are you ready?"

"Yep, but you ain't riding with us, Daddy." Cowboy's eyebrows raised in question and Brianna pointed to the red Cadillac CTS that was parked beside her SUV. "That's your ride there."

Cowboy looked at the Cadillac. He walked over to the passenger side of the car. The limousine tint was so dark that he couldn't see an outline of the driver. The window rolled down and Lorraine smiled at him.

"Lala?" Cowboy said, matching her smile.

"So you gonna stand there or you gonna get in your car?" Lorraine said, unlocking the door.

"My car?" Cowboy said as he opened the door.

"Yeah, this is a gift from your daughter." Lorraine said as she leaned over to kiss Cowboy.

Cowboy caressed her face, he looked into her eyes, and kissed her lips.

Brianna knocked on the window. "Ok you two, tone it down! I gotta go handle some business. So Daddy, when Mama let you come up for air, we can have dinner, okay?"

Cowboy and Lorraine beamed at Brianna. She touched her mother's face. It was the first time she had ever seen a genuine smile from her mother. Her heart felt warm, seeing her mother beam with love for her father. The man who in just a few short months had almost repaired the twenty-four years of emotional abuse she suffered from Herman. Thinking of that man's name seemed to make her head spin for a moment. Brandon wrapped his arms around Brianna's waist as they watch Cowboy and Lorraine pull out onto the street.

Herman looked around nervously before sticking his key in the door and entering his house. He hadn't been there in days, and he really wasn't sure what to expect since he had dug up Tank's body and moved it out of the backyard.

"Lorraine!" he yelled out, closing the door behind him, but not moving for a moment to see if she answered him.

Cautiously, he began to walk through the house, making sure that he was alone before he got comfortable. He called out Lorraine's name again as he climbed up the stairs, but still there was no answer. From the looks of their bedroom, Lorraine had not been home for a few days as well. He walked over to the dresser to grab a change of clothes, as he was about to take a quick shower. When he turned around to head to the bathroom, he was startled by Brianna, who was standing in the threshold of his bedroom door. She stood there with a Glock 9mm in her hand down by her waist, and her facial expression said that she wasn't in the mood to play any games.

"What did you do with the body, Herman?" she asked, tapping the gun on the side of her leg.

"Ah! That's for me to know and for you to find out," he responded with a devious grin on his face.

"I am not gonna ask you twice," she said, raising the gun and pointing it at his face.

Herman did not show any signs of fear, and that's probably because he wasn't scared at all. He knew that Brianna wasn't going to shoot him as long as she didn't get the information she was asking for. The options that he had with Tanks body were vast. He could plant that body anywhere, and all it would take was one phone call to the right homicide detective, and somebody was going to jail. Hell, if he played his cards right, he might be able to kill two birds with one stone. Something that he had already took into consideration.

"You're not going to shoot me..." Herman said in a calm voice. "I know that you're not gonna shoot me because if you do, you, yo mother, and ya punk ass daddy are going to jail for life. What do you think that I dug up the body for... my health?" he said, making his way across the room towards his closet.

Brianna thought about what he had said, especially the part where he threatened to put her mother in jail. That little comment made her nice and mad. Her gun stayed locked on him the whole time and she was two seconds away from shooting him until she thought about it. He did have the upper hand right now. That dead body could be anywhere, and who knows what other kind of tricks he had up his sleeves.

"Where's the body, Herman?" Brianna asked, watching him with a close eye while he rambled around in the closet.

"It's somewhere safe. And after I get what I want for it, you can have it."

"And what do you want for it?" Brianna asked, trying to figure out his angle, and at the same time, not lowering her gun.

Herman looked back over his shoulder to see Brianna still standing by the door with her gun pointed at him. The whole time that he was in the closet, he was waiting for the perfect opportunity to make his move. The three-foot long shotgun rested in the corner of the closet away from where Brianna could see it.

"To be honest with you Brianna ... I just want you to die." Herman said, grabbing the shotgun.

He spun around with it, cocking a slug into the chamber in the process. By the time Brianna noticed the gun, he was letting off a shot. Booom! Chit, chit!

Brianna dipped out of the room in the nick of time, avoiding the blast that knocked a hole in the wall the size of a basketball. She returned fire, sending a couple of shots through the hallway wall that was connected to his room. She was hoping that one of the bullets would hit him, but neither of them did. She backed down the hallway cautiously, facing his bedroom so that Herman wouldn't jump out and shoot her in the back.

Herman never came out of the room. Instead, he reached around and stuck the twelve gauge into the hallway. Brianna saw the long, black nose of the shotgun and fired two shots at it as she dropped to the ground.

Herman squeezed the trigger at the same time, blasting pieces of wood from the banister into Brianna's face. She crawled on her elbows backwards into the back room and slid behind the partition.

"I'ma fuckin kill you, Herman!" Brianna yelled out as she rose to her feet with her back against the wall.

"You know what they used to call me back in the day?" Herman taunted back, cocking another slug into the camber. "They used to call me, DOA. Cause I used to leave muthafuckas dead on arrival!" he yelled out, coming out of the room and looking down the hallway.

He didn't know what room Brianna was in, so he eased down the hallway with the shotgun at chest level. He kicked the bathroom door in and pointed the gun inside. Brianna peaked around, saw the opportunity, and opened fire. Herman found himself falling into the bathroom for cover while Brianna ran the short distance down the hall towards the steps. She continued to fire into the bathroom all the while, darting down the steps.

At this point, all she wanted to do was get out of the house, feeling that the gun battle wouldn't go in her favor. She wasn't sure how many more shots she had in her clip, nor did she know how much ammo

Herman had access to. It was either stay and risk being killed or flee and live to fight another day. Brianna choose the latter, taking off out the front door and dashing down the street to her waiting car.

Brianna got out of the car, and rushed inside the house. Selena and Chatima were sitting in the living room enjoying the latest episode of Love and Hip Hop Atlanta.

"Hey girl, what's going on with you?" Selena greeted Brianna, noticing her uneasiness.

"Is everything alright?" Chatima asked also, seeing the angry look that Brianna had on her face when she entered the home.

"Herman just tried to kill me." Brianna said, pulling Selena into the dining room away from Chatima and the noise of the television.

"He did what?" Selena responded with a shocked look on her face.

"Yeah, he tried to end me with a 12 gauge shotgun about an hour ago. Have you talked with Charrise?" she asked, looking around.

"Nah, I haven't talked to her in a couple of days. I been tryin' to call her phone but it goes straight to voicemail. Why? What's going on?" she asked, seeing the concerned look in Brianna's eyes. "Brianna, girl you need to calm yourself down, while we figure out, how we going to handle Herman's old ass." She pulled her phone out of her pocket and began searching for a number.

"Who you calling?" Brianna asked.

"I'm calling Gwen to let her know we going to have to postpone the sit down today. You're in no shape for that shit today!" Selena answered while still looking at the phone screen.

"No, don't cancel. It's a perfect day for the meet, because we about to handle all family business. I might as well start with her and start today!"

Herman walked out of the police station smiling. After Brianna's attempt to take his ass out, he needed to make sure that if that was to happen, she and everyone she loved would live to regret it. He had given Detective Hampton just enough information to pique his interest, but not enough to move on Brianna and Cowboy. He didn't want to play his hand too quickly. He needed to milk the situation for as much as he could.

He laughed as he closed the door of his car and took out his phone.

Cowboy lay on the bed stroking his hand up and down Lorraine's bare back. She rested her head on the pillow next to him, exhausted from Cowboy giving her something that she had missed for so many years. The way that Cowboy put his thing down in the bedroom was nothing less than spectacular. He made love, then fucked, then made love to Lorraine all over again. He made her reach peaks that Herman never could, and that was all done without the blue pill.

"You woke?" Cowboy whispered, looking down at her.

"Barely," she whispered back with a smile on her face.

"I miss you, LaLa," Cowboy confessed, calling her by the old nickname that he had given her back in the day.

Lorraine smiled at him as she laid her head on his chest. She could not remember the last time she had felt this happy, or this safe. Not since the last time she was in Cowboy's arms, but she had chosen to do the right thing by staying in her marriage as a good southern woman does. Her heart always ached for Cowboy because every time she looked into Brianna's eyes, she would see Cowboy. After being with him, she knew what total fulfillment was, and every day without him was empty. Herman could look at Lorraine and tell that he had lost her, which only fueled his hatred for Brianna. Looking at her had reminded him of what he had lost with Lorraine. She was a symbol of love between Cowboy and his wife.

"It's not too late for us, is it?" Lorraine said, kissing Cowboy's chest softly.

"No baby, it is never too late. You are where you should have been all along. I loved you enough to let you go, Lorraine, but this time I ain't going nowhere." Cowboy said, pulling her closer to him, and tasting her lips. As he kissed her, his hand slid down her stomach to her smooth pussy. He found her throbbing clit, and massaged it with his thumb.

Lorraine moaned and pushed him back on the bed. She straddled his lap and rubbed the large head of his dick against her clit, making it grow and harden with each stroke. He closed his eyes as he felt her slide down slowly on his dick. Cowboy's large wide dick was difficult for most women to take all at once, but Lorraine bit her lip and found her rhythm.

"Shit, baby." she said as she slid her hot creamy pussy up and down his pole.

Cowboy dug his nails into her fat ass because Lorraine knew how to please him, she always had. He opened his eyes to see her fat pussy lips making his dick shine with its cream.

"Damn Lala... ride Daddy right." Cowboy said as he squeezed her breasts together and pulled on her nipples. She bucked faster, causing the springs of the bed to squeak.

"Ohh... umm... ohhhhhh I love you!"

Cowboy felt her walls tighten around his dick. Lorraine threw her head back and slammed against him, as she grabbed his chest. Within moments, her box flooded all over his pole. Lorraine shivered and Cowboy lifted his hips to meet her thrusts. Her pussy throbbed, and sucked him in deeper. She collapsed on top of him, riding the high of her orgasm.

"Oh, you think we done?" Cowboy said as he flipped Lorraine over on her back.

Lorraine giggled, ready for another round with him in control. Her cell phone rang and she sighed. Cowboy grinned at her and handed her the phone.

"You know that is probably our child." Cowboy said as he kissed Lorraine's forehead and walked into the bathroom.

Lorraine looked that the screen. Seeing it was a blocked number, she was going to let it go to voice mail, but thought about Charrise. They had not heard from her in days, and she did not want to take the chance of missing her finally checking in.

"Hello?" Lorraine answered, looking up at the ceiling.

"You know, if we were in an Islamic country, you could be stoned to death for committing adultery." Herman said into the phone. "When I am done with you, you probably gonna wish you were stoned. You ain't shit, but you know what? I ain't even mad at your ass. We been done for a while, so it don't matter who you give that raggedy pussy to." Herman said laughing.

Lorraine lost the high of her orgasm immediately. Hearing his voice quickly destroyed her ecstasy within seconds.

"What do you want, Herman?" Lorraine asked as Cowboy walked out of the bathroom.

Cowboy sat down on the bed and motioned for her to hand him the phone.

"At least he got you in a nice hotel." Herman said, looking around the lobby of the Renaissance Hotel where Cowboy had taken her for the night. "Put ya fuckin boyfriend on the phone," he demanded, taking a swig of a cold beer he had brought along.

"What you want, nigga?" Cowboy said sitting on the edge of the bed.

"I see that you're enjoying my wife..." Herman began. "You think you just gone walk in and take my life, nigga? Well, you can have dem fucking hoes, but if you want dem and yo ass to be able to enjoy the free air outside a 6x9, you gonna need to pay me for my pain and suffering." Cowboy sighed and listened to Herman's slurred speech. "Tell ya daughter she better give me a mil by tomorrow afternoon. If I ain't got my money, the police will have this body." Herman said, sucking down the last of his beer as he sat down in one of the mahogany colored leather chairs.

"Damn, you's a fool, mafucka." Cowboy said, shaking his head. "Ain't nobody gonna give you shit, nigga."

"Oh yeah. Well I'ma make sure all ya mafuckas go to jail about this body." Herman threatened. "Have my fuckin bread by tomorrow or get ya front door kicked in by Charlotte's finest!" Herman yelled.

"Like I said, fuck you nigga, and we ain't given yo trifling ass shit!" Cowboy said hitting end and slinging the phone on the bed.

He stood quickly and began putting on his clothes. Lorraine slid her top over her head and walked over to Cowboy. She took his face in her hands and kissed his lips. She could tell whatever Herman had said to Cowboy had affected him, and she could see worry through the anger in his eyes.

"What did he say, baby?" Lorraine asked softly. Cowboy shook his head and slid on his pants. "Cowboy, what did he say?" she said again.

"He wants money baby... money in exchange to not go to the police about the body. This nigga asking for a million dollars." Cowboy said laughing as he put on his shoes.

Lorraine fell on the bed; her mind was racing. Herman was a ruthless and cruel man. She had stayed with him all these years out of a sense of tradition and what was right. It was time she stood up for her family and herself. She deserved to be happy, and she was going to be.

Brianna and Selena pulled up in front of Bravo's restaurant at Northlake mall. Gwen had chosen the location and Brianna the time. They had decided it would be best to leave Chatima at the house, just in case. Although the situation had some tension, both women were hoping that the whole thing was a simple misunderstanding. Gwen and Diamond were already seated and eating when Brianna and Selena sat down. Brianna didn't waste any time, and got right down to business.

"So what's this I hear about someone trying to cut me out of something I put together, trying to help their hungry ass out?" Brianna asked with a raised eyebrow.

"Look Brianna, we all just trying to eat out here, you can understand that, can't you?" Gwen responded while pointing at the plate of pasta she was feasting on.

"Ladies, how about you order you some food and let's eat first before we get down to the business," Diamond suggested.

"We're not hungry, thank you." Brianna responded.

"You see, and there lies the problem, Brianna. You not hungry anymore. You happy with just getting your money and letting things be. But it's a new day, Bri... A new era is here and women are at the top of the food chain in North Carolina. We trying to take over this shit, and I'ma be real wit you, because I really appreciate everything you and Selena done for me during my time of trouble. See this ain't just about me, this about my family, MHB, and I gots to do the best thing possible for them because I swore my life to this shit." Gwen said while pointing at her MHB tattoo.

"Well, I like the way you showing your appreciation." Brianna shot back sarcastically.

"Again, Brianna, it's not about me and you know what I'm saying is real. The truth is, me and my crew got this city on smash. So before me and you eventually bump heads, I wanna give you the option to get down wit my team." Gwen said, crossing her hands on the table.

"And what team is this supposed to be?" Brianna asked with an attitude. She was becoming a little irritated with the hidden ultimatum Gwen put out there like she wasn't going to catch on.

"Wait a minute, ladies..." Selena cut in, seeing that it was getting a little heated between the two women. From the way Brianna and Gwen stared at each other, she could tell that this was going to lead to something much more serious if they didn't calm down.

"Gwen, can you agree that it was kinda fucked up that you let Bri set up the meeting with Ana, and then you went behind her back?" Selena asked in a sincere tone, hoping to get some order back to the conversation.

"Like I said, Selena, that was not my intention. I told Brianna that we got trap houses and street dealers that need to be fed. I don't have time to wait for her to make moves so I can keep my family straight. So since she wasn't returning my calls, I went to the source. I was still going to give her something for the hook up, and I'm offering her and you a chance to get down with my crew."

"Gwen, baby how you going to offer me a chance when I'm the one that gave you one, and maybe that was a bad decision on my part. But don't worry, I won't be making any more of those. Oh, and remember you not the only one with an army or crew. Other people do have guns, missy." Brianna responded.

Diamond and Selena looked at each other, knowing that they had two egotistical women. So when it came to defending their reputations on the street, both would fight to the bitter end. Brianna felt like she was being pressed to get down with Gwen's crew or collide with her in the future if she declined. She took it more like a threat than anything. Truth was, Gwen wasn't making threats; she was merely speaking facts. Her crew did have the city in a headlock, and it was only a matter of time before her and Brianna's teams crossed paths. Brianna had wanted to fall back and MHB was pressing on the accelerator. For now, the best thing Selena and Diamond could do was separate the women and try to fix things at a later date, because right now, too much had been said. Tempers were flaring to the point where talking things out was about to be out the door.

Brianna left the meeting with an attitude. Nothing had been settled, and she still needed to deal with Herman's ass.

"And who da fuck is she to be talking about her city and her crew got it on smash," Brianna snapped, looking out onto the road as she drove down the street. "I never heard of no MHB. And why da fuck are you worried about what blocks I run?" she continued, smacking the steering wheel. Selena didn't speak a word. She knew Brianna was just venting and really didn't want an answer to the questions she was spewing. Brianna's phone ringing was the only thing that kept her from talking to herself the whole ride.

"Hey Daddy," she said as she put her earplugs in.

"We got a problem. Where are you at?" Cowboy spoke.

"I'm on the block dealing with another issue." Brianna said looking back at the trap house, she was pulling up in front of. She wanted to make sure everyone in her crew was on point, just in case shit took a turn before her and Gwen could get it worked out.

"Well, we got another predicament. I need you to meet me at the gas station on Statesville road in about twenty minutes, and make sure you are strapped, baby girl. Watch yourself." Cowboy said before ending the call.

Brianna sighed. She needed things to calm down. She had not known her father long, but Cowboy was cold as ice, and it would take a lot to unnerve him. She could hear stress in his voice, and if there was stress in it, it had to involve Herman. She hadn't heard from his lame ass since their shoot out. *Not hearing from him was just as bad as hearing from his stupid ass,* she thought to herself. It just meant he was cooking up some damn scheme. He was probably waiting for the right moment to strike. She should have put a bullet between his eyes when she had the chance. He should have joined Tank in that damn hole. Brianna placed the car back in drive and changed direction, heading for Statesville road. *Damn,* she thought to herself. She could only handle one problem at a time, and right now, she really needed to be handling her money and block.

Gator was relaxing in the bathtub. The last lick Jonathan and his crew had taken down had yielded some good cash. Now, she was in need of drugs if she was going to keep her South Carolina and Detroit connection going well. She had to make sure Jonathan and them found some new victims quick, and they needed to hit the house before the drugs had been exchanged for money. She texted Jonathan to come home as quickly as possible. She had a crazy night of sex planned for them both. She knew how to keep her young pup motivated, and tonight she was planning to take him to the next level of his sex game.

A.J. pulled on the weed as he sat two blocks away from Betty Ford Rd, the same place where Jonathan brought him before the lick to do his research. Kevin's death wasn't sitting right with him and the only thing that could ease the pain was getting revenge. Jonathan killing one female in the warehouse wasn't enough. More needed to be done, and A.J. was up for putting in the work, even if it was by himself.

"These bitches got a nigga fucked up," A.J. said, exhaling the weed smoke.

The whole car was cloudy. A.J. reached over and grabbed his cell phone out of the center console. He didn't know whether he was going to make it out of there alive, so he decided to call Jonathan, just in case.

"Yo, what it do, homie?" Jonathan answered, looking over at Gator who gave him a look like he better not even think about leaving the house.

"Aye yo, I miss my nigga," A.J. spoke into the phone. "He didn't deserve dat shit, homie," he said, almost bringing himself to tears.

Jonathan could see the combination of alcohol and weed all in A.J.'s speech. He knew that A.J. was still having a tough time coping with the loss of Kevin. He just didn't know to what extent.

"It's gonna be alright, Brah, just tell me where you are, so I can come and get you." Jonathan said, not wanting A.J. to be riding around high and drunk.

"I'm out here, Brah. I am about to take care of these bitches," he responded, taking another puff of the weed. "All these bitches gonna die," he said, reaching back and grabbing the AR-15 off the back seat.

He put the phone on speaker and sat it on the dash, so that he could talk and smoke weed, while he admired the beauty of the assault rifle that was sitting on his lap at the same time.

"A.J., don't do nothing stupid, Brah," Jonathan spoke, worried that he might have been too late. "Just tell me where you're at my nig, so that I can come and get you," Jonathan pleaded.

"Yo, I love you, my nigga" A.J. said, cocking a bullet into the chamber of the large gun.

Jonathan knew that sound all too well, and he knew that if A.J. had gotten that far, it wasn't no turning back. He couldn't try and talk him out of it if he wanted to, and before he could even attempt to, the phone went dead.

Chapter 11

Chatima lay bored on the couch. She had been watching nothing but TV all day, and was wondering if coming to visit her big cousin in North Carolina was a good idea. She took out her phone to check the time. Before she placed it on the table, the name Selena came up with a buzz. She had just thought her up.

"Yo, what's up, cuz?" she asked.

"Nothing much, I just wanted to touch base with you and let you know it will be a little while before we get back. Also, I need you to do something for me, to put my mind at ease."

"Sure cuzzo, what's up? What you need?" Chatima asked, unsure what she could provide to calm her cousin's mind.

"I need you to go into my room and grab the large black Gucci backpack and take it down to the basement. When you get to the wall on the far left side, let me know."

Chatima did has she was instructed, and when she got to the wall, she pressed all the necessary buttons to get the secret door panel to move aside, revealing a stash room. The small six by nine room contained ammunition, a selection of guns, money and more product. Selena told her to leave the bag in there. She and Brianna weren't sure what Herman had told the cops. So as a precaution, they didn't want large sums of money or drugs lying around in the house if the cops decided to show up.

"Done, big cuz. Is there anything else I can do for you?" Chatima asked.

"No, that's it. Thank you, sweetie, and I promise, we going to hang out all day tomorrow together, ok?" Selena reassured Chatima.

"You promise?"

"I promise!"

"Ok, talk to you later." Chatima hung up the phone.

As she stepped out of the room, she paused. A chill ran down her spine; she felt like she wasn't alone. A sour smell drifted to her nostrils. She began to reach for a gun she saw on the shelf back in the room, but something hit her hard in the back of her head.

Chatima screamed as she fell to the floor. Her vision was blurry for a moment. She tried to reach up to grab something to help her stand, but suddenly she couldn't breathe. The sour smell was right on top of her, covering her face. She continued trying to get up.

"Come here bitch!" Chatima felt something slice into the back of her knee, and then an arm was around her neck. She tried to elbow him, but he lifted her off the floor and continued to apply pressure to her windpipe. She felt four more stabs; the second stab caused her body to become paralyzed. He had jabbed the blade into her back. Tears ran down her face, as she felt the darkness surround her.

"Yeah bitch, that's right, die." Herman said as he tightened the chokehold and slid the blade one last time into her back before letting her limp body fall to the floor.

Herman kicked Chatima and she didn't move. He turned on the light and walked into the small room. Chatima hadn't had time to close the door. Herman stood there and smacked his hands together while laughing.

"Hell yeah!" He looked at the dope and guns.

Herman spotted the large black duffle bag in the corner. He unzipped it and took out a stack of money. There had to be at least 100K in the bag. Herman laughed and kissed the bundle of money. He was about to leave when he realized that one of the guns on the table could have been the one used to kill Tank. Damn, at first he had thought that coming to Brianna's house was a bad idea, but now it could be really paying off for him.

Brianna and Selena pulled into the Pilot gas station on Statesville Ave. Cowboy was waiting at pump three like he was getting some gas, and cautiously checking his surroundings for any signs of danger. He didn't trust Herman one bit. That's why he kept Lorraine close by him, and he wasn't going to let her out of his sight.

"Hey Dad," Brianna said, after rolling her window down. "Is my Mom in the car with you?" she asked, not getting out of the truck.

"Yeah, she's good, but check dis out. Dat nigga Herman called ya Mom's phone talking about how he wants you to pay him a million dollars for Tank's body or he is putting all of us in jail." Cowboy explained.

"What did you tell him?" Brianna asked.

"I told dat nigga we wasn't giving him shit. I don't have a million dollars to give dat nigga." Cowboy responded. "Plus, that summabitch want dat shit by tomorrow afternoon." he added.

Brianna leaned her head against the steering wheel and took in a deep breath. She didn't even have a million in cash right now, especially with the moves Gwen was making.

"I'ma need a couple of days to get that together," Brianna spoke. "If he calls back, give him my number and tell him to call me. Take my Mom over to Jonathan's and then meet me back at my house. I'ma get the million dollars, but I guarantee Herman won't be able to spend a dime of it," she said, looking down at her phone.

"If it's all the same to you, baby, I'ma keep your mom near me. I'll take her back to my house."

Brianna smiled. She waved to her mom before rolling up her window and pulling off with nothing but murder on her mind.

Brandon sat in his car in front of Brianna's house waiting for her to get home. He had a lot on his mind and he wanted to talk to her seriously about their relationship and her lifestyle. Brandon stretched and got out of his car, he heard the engine of Brianna's truck as she pulled into the driveway and opened her garage. Brandon smiled at her as she opened the door of her car and grabbed her bag.

"Hey Brandon, I really don't have a lot of time to talk right now," Brianna said as she hit the garage door button, and opened the door to the house. Her and Selena walked through the laundry room, into the kitchen, and stopped. Brandon was about to say something when he walked into the back of both them.

"Shh." Brianna said as she looked around the kitchen.

She placed her bag on the table and grabbed her gun. She motioned for Selena to go around the dining room and secure upstairs. She then told Brandon to stay back as she walked into the living room. The door to the basement was open, which made Brianna's blood run cold. She ran down the stairs and stopped short when a heavy metallic smell filled her nostrils.

"Chatima?" she called out in the dark space. When she got no response, she turned on the overhead light. "Chatima! Oh God!" Brianna yelled as she ran over to where she laid. "Brandon call 911!"

"Selena, get down here!" Brianna yelled.

Selena ran down the stairs and saw Brianna standing over Chatima's body.

"No Bri, tell me that's not my little cousin! No... no... no...That's not my Tima... Please God, no!"

Selena kept screaming while walking around. She was refusing to believe she had brought her baby cousin down there to lose her life.

Brianna kept her gun drawn. She walked into the basement and slowly opened the door to her stash room. Her cash was gone, along with some guns. She cursed, now was not the time for her to lose any money at all. She closed the door and slid the rack back in front of the access.

"Is she still alive? The ambulance is on its way." Brandon said as he leaned over and placed his ear to Chatima's mouth.

"Chatima! Chatima! Please, just hold on, cuz!" Selena was screaming, hoping the loud sound of her voice would bring her cousin back to life. She leaned over Chatima's lifeless body and began CPR.

Brianna looked at her friend. She knew that it was too late for Chatima, but she didn't have the heart to pull Selena off her. Instead, she kneeled down, grabbed one of Selena's hands and placed her other hand over Chatima's face to close her eyes. Brianna knew who was responsible for this, and as she sat there holding Selena's hand, her blood boiled. Herman was going to pay, and he was going to pay with his life.

Cowboy felt a chill come over his body as he approached Brianna's house. The street was covered with EMTs, and police officers. He opened the door without putting the car in park; it rolled against the curb and stopped. He ran through the crowd that had gathered and attempted to enter the front door of the house.

"This is my daughter's house!" Cowboy yelled as he struggled to get past the police officers.

Brianna heard Cowboy struggling and walked to the door. "Hold up, that's my dad!" Brianna yelled to the officers trying to stop Cowboy from entering the house.

Cowboy sighed with relief when he saw and heard Brianna. He ran to her and hugged her. "Are you okay baby girl?" he said as he looked down at the pool of blood on the floor. The room was full of detectives, and flashes were going off as forensic people took pictures of the living room.

"Yeah, yeah, I am fine, but..." Brianna paused as she looked at the floor. She fought back tears as she thought of Chatima's last moments. "Selena's cousin, Chatima is dead. I'm convinced Herman stabbed her to death, and I will know for sure once I can view the surveillance equipment."

Brianna buried her face in Cowboy's chest. Cowboy looked back at the blood on the floor as he walked Brianna into the kitchen. Brianna could see the concern on his face as the police were walking through the house.

"Nothing is here, Daddy. Herman pretty much took everything, and the stash room is not something the cops will find easily. If they do, there is nothing there illegal." Selena had already taken everything and left before the cops arrived.

"How much did he take?" Cowboy asked as he poured a glass of water for Brianna.

"Let's go out back," she suggested.

He followed Brianna to the backyard. She looked back to see where the detectives were as she sat down in the blue patio chair.

"He made out with about 300K and a couple of kilos, some guns, and worst of all, he got the gun used in the Tank incident." Brianna buried her face in her hands.

Cowboy took a deep breath. Herman was an issue before, but now he had two pieces of evidence that could end all of their lives. Cowboy wasn't afraid of going to prison, but he didn't want his daughter to have that life. He was not going to watch his baby be put in a cage. Life had kept her away from him for twenty-four years. He was not going to lose another day with her, due to a bastard like Herman.

Brianna's phone buzzed. She looked at the screen. The number showed as private. She was hoping it was Charrise.

"Yeah?"

"Hey little bitch, how ya friend doing?" Herman said as he took a swig of his cold beer. "Little bitch had some fight in her, but when I put that hold on her ass, it was lights out!"

Brianna looked at Cowboy, her jaw tightened as Herman taunted her. "Well, enough of that shit... you gots til noon to get me the rest of my money... or you and your hoeing ass mama and punk ass Daddy gonna be wearing wardrobes designed by the state!"

"I hate you."

"Well that ain't no way to talk to the man who raised you... you ungrateful little bitch!"

"You ain't did shit, nigga. Why did you kill that girl? She ain't had nothing to do with this."

"She got in my way, and cause I could take her ass out, just like I can take yo ass down. Now have my money!"

The line clicked, and Brianna's head began to pound. She wanted to scream, but she covered her mouth and bit the inside of her hand.

"That was that nigga?" Cowboy asked, already knowing the answer.

Brianna shook her head. Cowboy and Brianna knew this had nothing to do with money. Killing Chatima was just his sick way of torturing Brianna, the way he had her entire life. He would not be satisfied until he had destroyed all of them, even his own children. Brianna stood as she looked up at the sky, and then went back into the house. She wasn't a kid anymore, and Herman was just flesh and blood. Brianna was going to make sure that blood spilled.

A.J. got out of the car and began walking down the street towards Betty Ford. He could see a nice crowd of females standing in the middle of the block serving what looked to be dope fiends. He kept the AR-15 down by his side until he got close enough to where it didn't matter if anybody saw it or not. When he got to the top of Betty Ford, he picked up his pace a bit, taking in mental notes of his surroundings. His fast walking pace turned into a light jog, and once he got within 15 yards of the women, he raised the AR-15 and let it rip right into the crowd.

It had to be at least five women and two men standing out there, all of whom scattered like roaches at the sounds of the automatic weapon.

"Arrggg!" one of the females yelled after taking a bullet to her leg.

Another female dropped to the ground and returned fire, forcing A.J. to duck behind a parked car. Other people from the block joined in the gun battle. A.J. jumped up from behind the car and let the AR-15 rip again.

He fired wildly up and down the street, not caring who he hit.

Others began shooting back at A.J., forcing him to again take cover behind the car. Bullets flew by his head and knocked holes in the car. The return fire got so loud that A.J. started to get worried. He peeked up over the passenger door to see people coming from everywhere with guns in their hands. It got to the point where he became scared instead of worried. He might have bitten off more than he could chew, messing with the Betty Ford chicks.

A.J. jumped up from behind the car, but this time with an exit strategy in mind. He fired off, backpedaling down the street towards his car. The AR-15 ran out of bullets, and the only thing that A.J. could do was take off running.

Two females from the block started to run after him, but were stopped. "Hold up, hold up... Let him go," Gwen said, whipping her phone out and punching in some numbers. "Somebody get me something to help stop the bleeding!" she yelled, running over to the young woman who had taken a bullet to the leg.

"We just gone let him go?" a female said, standing there with a gun in her hand, watching A.J. fade away into the dark night.

"Yeah, now get over here and hold this on the wound," Gwen responded while getting up with the phone still on her ear.

"Yo!" she spoke to the person on the other end of the phone. "Alright, say no more," she said, hanging up the phone, satisfied with what she had just heard from the person she was talking to.

Gwen looked up the street and smiled. She was expecting that to happen eventually. Her street knowledge was impeccable, and she knew that it was only a matter of time before somebody was going to retaliate for Kevin's death, even after they killed the female at the stash house. It was only right. Gwen would have done the same thing if it was somebody close to her. It had become personal, and it was shown by the way that the gunman came through. The dude wasn't trying to rob anybody. He didn't even have any prior altercations with anybody that day, and when he let his gun spray, she could hear the hurt in his voice.

Gwen might have been a female, but she peeped game and was on point like a sniper the second that the first shot was let off. Now, feeling the same way that A.J. felt, it was time for Gwen to retaliate too, but her way of retaliating was far worse than anything A.J. could imagine. She definitely was a problem.

Jonathan sat on the couch and smiled at the text message he was reading. Gator had gone out of town to check on some family she had in South Carolina. At least, that was the story she told him. It was the first serious time they had been apart since getting together, and he was missing her like crazy. She had come in and turned his whole world upside down. Gator had forced him to grow up quickly and become a man. He looked in the mirror, admiring his latest tattoo of praying hands with a scroll that read, "RIP Big Kev." Both he and A.J. had gotten one in remembrance of their fallen homie.

Gator texted him back a message with two hearts combined as one, representing their love. She also promised to make her time away up to him as soon as she returned. Jonathan thought about how sweet her pussy tasted in his mouth and had to adjust his growing member. He looked out the window when he heard an engine idling close to the house. He saw A.J. sitting in his car with his head tilted back.

Jonathan grabbed the blue steel glock and walked out the door with it by his side. The driver's window was down. He checked A.J., and found him asleep with his foot on the brake. He could smell the alcohol on him. He opened the door, put the car in park, and turned off the engine.

"A.J… A.J. wake up man, come on inside." A.J. snorted and slowly opened his eyes.

Jonathan pulled him out the car and help him inside. Once inside, Jonathan led A.J. to the couch, A.J. fell onto the couch and moaned.

"Man, where you coming from?"

A.J. laughed and attempted to sit up. "I had to get dem bitches for what they did to Kevin, man. I lit dey asses up." Jonathan looked out the window again.

"Man, what you mean? You lit them up?" Jonathan asked.

A.J. laughed and made shooting sounds.

Jonathan walked out and looked up and down the block. He hit the garage door opener and pulled A.J.'s car inside. The state that A.J. was in, Jonathan knew that he could have been followed, and he didn't need that kind of shit at his front door right now. He walked back inside after closing the garage door. A.J. was snoring on the couch.

Jonathan sat down in the recliner, and watched his friend sleep. He had at least gotten the satisfaction of taking one of the bitches out in the warehouse, but A.J. hadn't gotten any satisfaction in hurting the people who had taken Kevin's life.

Jonathan's phone whistled again, it was a message from Gator. A.J. turned over on the couch and began to snore loudly.

Look, when I get back, I'm going to really need you to have some white girls waiting on me. And don't fuck this up!

Jonathan sighed and smiled. Gator had him mesmerized for the moment. She was a grown ass woman, and he knew that if he wanted to play with her, he needed to leave the boy shit at home and man up for her. Giving her good dick was not going to be enough to keep her interested, and he didn't want to be just some boy toy. Yeah, he knew he would need to make sure he had some dope waiting on her return. He had to earn her respect in and out of the bedroom.

Selena swayed back and forth on her stool to the music she had selected from the Juke Box in the corner of the bar. One shot glass and a bottle of Patron sat in front of her, and after throwing back three shots of the clear fire water, she was beginning to feel its effects. Tina, the bartender, and good friend of the family, monitored Selena's drinking very closely and knew that within two more shots, she would have to come over and confiscate the bottle from her. She had heard through the grapevine about her cousin, Chatima, so she gave her a little space to unwind.

"Are you alright, baby girl?" Tina asked, checking up on her. "You know if you need to talk to somebody, I am right here."

"Yeah, I'm good. Just don't take my bottle." Selena chuckled, wrapping both hands around the bottle of Patron and hugging it like it was her best friend.

Tina smiled and then walked over to attend to one of her other customers. Selena looked at herself in the mirror behind the bar and couldn't help but to think about her little cousin. The liquor played a major part in her thought process right now, so it was no surprise that she went back to some of her old childhood memories when they were just some innocent little girls. She thought about the times when they used to play jump rope with the other girls on the block, and how being her big cousin meant she had to protect her. Those were the happier times in her life that she wanted so desperately to go back to. Now she was faced with the task of calling back to her aunt Shirley and giving her the news of her only child's death. A death that she was responsible for. One that Brianna was even more responsible for. Why hadn't Brianna already killed Herman? Maybe she was becoming soft, like Gwen had said. Shit, her weakness had cost her cousin her life...

Selena could slightly hear her phone ringing in her bag as the song on the jukebox was going off. She reached inside and pulled out the iPhone to see that it was Brianna calling her. Just like all day yesterday, she didn't answer it. Instead, this time she turned her phone off altogether. She really didn't feel like being bothered by nobody right now.

"Damn, I see you got some shit on ya mind to," a voice said from behind.

Selena looked up in the mirror and could see the reflection of a familiar face looking back at her. She looked to see Gwen, who pulled out a stool and took a seat in it. *Damn, did I just think her up?* Selena thought to herself.

"Yeah, it's always some shit." Selena responded.

"Tina... get me another shot glass and a few slices of lemon," Gwen instructed.

"You know Tina?" Selena asked, checking Gwen out.

"Of course I know Tina. From the way she got her eyes on you, it looks like you were about one shot away from her taking that bottle away from you." Gwen smiled.

"Me and Tina gonna be fighting up in here if she thinks that she is taking this bottle from me."

They shared a laugh at the thought. Tina walked over and put the shot glass on the table in front of Gwen, smiling at Selena's comment that she overheard.

"Shit, I just lost a good friend, so I know how you feel. But let me ask you something... Why is Brianna tripping about a sister trying to come up and handle her business?" Gwen asked, pouring a shot into her glass.

Selena had to think about the question. After pondering it for a moment, she came up with the only answer that was feasible.

"Gwen, you got to be honest, she introduces you to her connect to help you out and then you back door her? Come on, you know that ain't right, and Brianna hardly likes anybody. She lives in her own world, so if she feels like she's not in control of a situation, she will shut you down in a New York minute." Selena said, tossing back her fourth shot. "What about you? What's your angle?"

"I really don't have an angle, except one, and that's FAMILY! Nothing and no one can come between or before that... you feel me? So no matter how much I like and appreciate what she did for me in my time of need, I can't use that has an excuse when it comes to doing what's best for my family first. Also, I just feel like us being women, we should be able to understand that and stick together. God knows that I am not anti-men, but I think we hold more power if we work as one unit," Gwen said, throwing back her second shot. "That's all that I was trying to explain to your people."

"Well, I think that you turned her off when you said that you run this city. Don't nobody run Brianna," Selena shot back.

"Well, what about you? What do you think?" Gwen asked.

"Well... I think that I had too much to drink because I am doing a little too much talking." Selena chuckled. She didn't want to tell her what she was really thinking. How she loved the love that Gwen had for family and how Gwen was willing to break any ties to make sure she put family first. Maybe if Brianna had those leadership qualities, Chatima would still be alive.

Both women sat there in silence for a minute. Tina kept a close eye on Selena's intake. When she went to pour another shot, Tina walked over and grabbed the bottle.

"That's five, baby girl. I gotta call you a cab," Tina said, walking over to the phone.

"No, no, it's cool, Tina," Gwen said, waving her hand. "She's cool. I will make sure to get her home safe." Gwen assured.

Tina didn't put up a fight. She knew that if Gwen said that she had her, then it was no doubt in her mind that Selena would be safe with her.

"How about it? You wanna take a ride with me?" Gwen asked, leaning over and nudging Selena.

"It sounds like I'ma regret it in the morning," Selena responded with a bit of slurred speech.

"Or, it might be the best thing that ever happened to you," Gwen shot back, standing up off her stool.

Drunk, but still aware of what was going on, Selena rose to her feet as well. She didn't feel a sense of a threat coming from Gwen, and at the same time, she was a bit curious to know exactly what Gwen was up to. In the event that Gwen did get stupid in the course of the night, Selena knew that her trusty sidekick sitting in her back would definitely see to it that a safe exit would be granted, no matter where she was. It was times like this that Selena appreciated keeping her gun on her.

Chapter 12

Brianna pulled up to Jonathan's house. She sighed as she thought of how she was going to break the news of Chatima's death to Kasy. She had texted him last night, but he didn't answer until this morning. She walked down the sidewalk to the front door. Taking a deep breath, she rang the doorbell.

"Hey, big sis!" Jonathan said as he hugged her.

Brianna smiled at Jonathan. Even though he had grown up, she still saw him as her baby brother who would follow her around the house, and play hide and seek.

"Hey handsome, how are you doing?" Brianna said as she placed her bag on the couch. "Damn, who in here cooking? I heard you got some old broad shacking up with you. Do I finally get to meet her today?" Brianna said as she followed him into the kitchen.

"Not today, but in due time, sis, in due time," Jonathan responded.

A.J. was sitting at the table with his head down. "What's wrong with A.J.?" Brianna asked Jonathan.

Jonathan laughed and pointed to the empty bottle of gin on the counter.

Brianna shook her head and thumped A.J. on the back of the neck. "Wake your punk ass up, light weight."

"Ahh, Bri, damn... my head already ringing." Brianna and Jonathan laughed.

Kasy was taking biscuits out of the oven and spraying butter on top of them. "What up Bri? Sit down and I will fix you a plate."

Brianna smiled and took a seat. She poured herself a glass of orange juice and checked her text messages. Kasy placed a plate in front of her and Jonathan. He grabbed the two other plates and sat down at the table.

"So, what's up, Bri? You said you wanted to talk to me about something."

"Yeah, let's eat first." Brianna said.

Kasy bowed his head and blessed the table. Jonathan and Kasy talked about the game. Brianna smiled and listened to their chatter as A.J. snored at the table.

"Look at this nigga." Kasy said, poking A.J. with his fork.

A.J. stood suddenly and ran to the bathroom.

"Eww... I'm glad he waited until we finished eating before hurling." Brianna said as she cleared the table and placed the dishes in the dishwasher. She stared out the window for a moment and then turned to look at Kasy and Jonathan.

"Aight guys... I have some bad news... Kasy," Brianna said as she walked over to the table. "Yesterday, me and Selena was out making some runs for some product for one of the trap houses. Well, we left Chatima at the house, and somehow Herman ambushed her...She was killed." Brianna squeezed the last part of her statement out as tears rolled down her face.

Kasy stared at her for a moment. Brianna held his hand, and pulled him close to her. His body was stiff and he did not make a sound.

"What you mean Herman killed her? Why, why would he do that, Brianna?" Jonathan asked.

Brianna sat down at the table.

A.J. stumbled out of the bathroom, and fell into one of the chairs.

"Why y'all looking like someone died?" A.J. said as he sipped some water.

"Chatima is dead, A.J." Jonathan said.

"What?" A.J. responded. "What? How?"

"Herman stabbed her to death." Brianna said looking at Kasy who had not said a word. "He must have followed her into the house, and waited for her to open the stash room."

"Herman did that? Why would he do something like that?"

"He is fucking bastard, man." Jonathan said as he stood. "A bastard that should be taking an eternal nap in the dirt."

"How you know it was Herman, Bri?" Kasy said through clenched teeth.

"He called me. He wants me to pay him a million dollars."

"For what?" Jonathan asked.

Brianna sighed and filled the three of them in on what Herman was using to blackmail her. The room was quiet when she finished telling them the details. Jonathan knew that Herman was the reason Charrise had been kidnapped. Now he had actually tried to kill Brianna, blackmailed her, and had murdered Chatima. Jonathan walked into the living room and grabbed his automatic.

"What the hell are you doing?" Brianna asked as she looked at him holding the gun. "What are you doing with that, Jonathan?"

"Somebody gotta handle Herman, Brianna… this nigga is out of control!"

"I said what are you doing with a gun, Jonathan?" Brianna asked again. She had no idea that her baby brother had turned into a ruthless murder and stick-up boy.

"Bri, I'ma go handle this dude."

Brianna stared at her brother holding the glock. How had this happened? When did this happen? This was her baby brother, a college kid. He was not this person she was staring at in front of her. Everyone stood silently in the living room. Jonathan dropped his head to avoid Brianna's eyes. He looked at A.J. who had sobered up.

"Y'all betta get to talking and I mean right now!" Brianna hadn't questioned why Kasy was at the house. He was cool with her family, but now that she thought about it, why the hell was he hanging out at Jonathan's?

A.J. cleared his throat and walked towards the front door. When he opened the door and walked outside, bullets zinged, and he fell back on the threshold. Bullets flew through the windows of the house.

Kasy pushed Brianna to the floor and grabbed the assault rifle that was under the couch. Bullets assaulted the house, causing glass to rain down on them.

Jonathan began firing back.

Brianna watched in amazement as her baby brother handled himself like a fucking soldier. Brianna grabbed her bag off the couch, took out her glock, and began firing through the window. She looked over at A.J. who laid half way in the house and out. "Who the fuck is shooting at you?"

Kasy crawled to the kitchen. He returned and threw an AR 16 to Jonathan. He began spraying. Brianna's car was being shredded by the gunfire, but that wasn't her concern at the moment. Brianna tried to see where the gunfire was coming from. She could see a black van, and a female firing shots into the house. Kasy had made his way into the master bedroom. Brianna saw a flash coming from the right side of the house and the female screamed as a bullet ripped through some part of her. Another female pulled her back inside the van and the van peeled off down the street.

Jonathan jumped up and stepped over A.J., and continued firing at the van as it sped off. Brianna crawled over to A.J., his chest rattled as he took a breath.

"Hey, no, A.J.! No, hold on! Baby, hold on!"

The sirens were approaching. Jonathan ran back towards the house. Blood ran down the side of A.J.'s mouth, and his body began to convulse.

"No brah... No! Hold on, man!" A.J.'s eyes turned to Jonathan, and that's where they stayed.

Jonathan screamed as he pulled A.J. into his arms. "No man... no, you can't leave me too! Come on man, wake up please! Please man!" Brianna's heart ached as she watched Jonathan shake A.J., and then rock back and forward with him in his arms.

Kasy grabbed the assault rifle from beside Jonathan and ran to the back of the house, just as the police pulled up in front of the home.

Brianna had no idea who the females were that shot up the house and had killed A.J., but she knew whoever it was would be dead very soon.

Selena walked out onto the balcony overlooking the city. The view was crazy from the 39th floor of the Arlington Condos. The interior design of the condo was modern and sexy. It had three large bedrooms, plus two and half baths. Each room had a view of Charlotte's skyline, and it had a balcony large enough to entertain fifteen to twenty people comfortably.

"You know, you can stay here as long as you want." Gwen said, as she walked out onto the terrace with Selena.

Selena smiled at Gwen. Over the last few days, the women had confided in each other. Selena had told Gwen about the death of her baby cousin. Gwen's heart ached as Selena talked, because she could feel her pain. She thanked her again for all her help and sympathy during the Zion situation. The women cried and leaned on each other. Although they had not known each other long, something between them had clicked. A stronger bond was formed.

"Oh, I almost forgot to tell you. I think that I might be able to help you out with ya situation. All I really need is the green light from you so some of my girls can move out on it," Gwen said, looking over at Selena.

Selena had told Gwen about her plans to murder Herman, and all she needed to do was locate him. She didn't want to give him a quick death; she wanted to make him suffer. She also wanted to make sure he died by her hands and her hands only.

"Yeah, we can move on that." Selena responded, not taking her eyes off the view.

"That's all I needed to hear." Gwen said, heading back into the condo.

"Where are you creeping off to?" Selena playfully said, walking back into the condo behind her.

"I got some business to take care of myself. A guy came through one of my blocks shooting the other day. One of my friends was shot and he damn near killed me too."

"Daaammm!" Selena said. "Do you know who it was?"

"Yeah, and already taken care of him, but I still got one more to go. That's why I gotta leave right now," she said, heading for the door.

"You need me to come with you?" Selena asked.

"Nah, I'm good. You just chill out for tonight and call me when you get up in the morning." Gwen said, before leaving.

Jonathan sat on the bed and stared at the ceiling fan as it turned. There was a knock at the door, then it opened. Lorraine walked in and climbed into the bed with her son. She knew no matter how much he tried to act like he was all grown up, he was still her baby boy, and right now he needed the love and comfort of his mother.

Jonathan tried to fight back the tears, but feeling his mother's arms around him made him feel safe, and secure. The tears began to flow. "I'm alone, Mama... my boys are gone. They gone." he said, holding on tightly to his mother.

Lorraine did not understand what had happened, and how two of Jonathan's closet friends ended up being murdered within weeks of each other. She wanted to grill Jonathan, but her heart wouldn't let her, so she decided to just be there for him. There would be plenty of time later to ask all the questions she had running through her mind. She had raised her children to be productive and progressive citizens. Her daughter was a drug dealer, along with her younger sister. Now the one child that she thought would have a normal life was drawn into something dangerous and dark too. Herman, who had always been a monster, was tormenting them all. Her family was in danger of being destroyed, and she had to figure out a way to stop it from happening.

Brianna and Kasy had made their way to the last of her trap houses. Kasy had disappeared after the shooting, but showed back up this morning. His being calm at the news of Chatima's death had made Brianna nervous. She looked over at him as she opened the door of her car to walk up to the trap house.

"Kasy, how you holding up?"

"I'm holding, sis," he said as he looked up and down the street. "I hope you know I'm gone kill yo step daddy." He said with a deadly glare.

Brianna laughed. "Well, you gonna have to get in line for that." she said as they approached the trap house.

Ivory walked over to the SUV that Gwen was sitting in. Gwen did not stop playing Candy Crush on her phone. Ivory stood silently while Gwen completed her round of the game. Gwen sighed and rolled the window down.

"So, what you got for me, Iv?"

"I know we got dude that shot up the block. He came out the house and ate some lead. He had on the same clothes he had on when he sprayed ya the other day. They had some firepower, and Boom took one to the shoulder. Dank is stitching her up right now. That was when we pulled out, and as we were leaving, a dude came out shooting."

Gwen looked at her manicured nails as Ivory talked. "So a dude came out shooting at you?"

"Yeah a young dude. I can't be sure that he is one of the one's that was at the condo."

"I'm sure that is our third nigga, and I want you to give the other license plate to our contact downtown. Once you get that info, I want you to take his ass out."

Ivory nodded. "Oh damn, I almost forgot to tell you, guess who else was there at the house."

"Who?" Gwen asked, looking at Ivory like 'bitch just tell me who.'

"Girlie from the sit down at the restaurant the other day."

Gwen raised up in the car. Ivory had piqued her interest.

"Which girl from the sit down?"

"The boss lady… the light skin long hair chick… the one you had the words with."

Gwen looked down and then back at Ivory, "Damn… ole girl Brianna got more balls than I thought. Look like she really might be about this life."

Gwen rolled the window up and started the SUV. Maybe this crew of young boys was some of Brianna's people. Had she really underestimated her? One thing she was sure of was this business was going to be over with soon. She was going to make sure of it. First, she had to make sure everyone in the city of Charlotte understood and respected the three letters her crew represented, or the morgue was going to be getting a lot more business.

"Alright, listen up guys. We will be meeting my C-I shortly. He states he knows where the body of a murder victim is, and he can lead us to the weapon. I don't want Mrs. Campbell and her father escaping this one." Detective Sanders said as he popped an antacid. "So nobody do shit unless you hear from me. Remember, these people are armed and dangerous." Sanders said as he passed a sheet with pictures of Cowboy, Brianna and Jonathan on it.

Sanders did not put too much into what Herman was saying at the beginning, due to the alcohol that reeked from him. Herman had explained to Sanders that this Tank guy owed Cowboy and Brianna money. They had kidnapped him and brought Tank to his house. Cowboy was a known hired gun, and his stepdaughter was a drug king pin. He was fearful of both of them. They tortured the man for hours, and then Brianna ordered Cowboy to kill hm. Herman said he had come home to find his son and Cowboy wrapping the body up. Brianna and Cowboy had threatened to kill him if he said anything to anyone.

Herman made sure his performance was Oscar worthy. He added that due to the stress of trying to keep this secret, he had been drinking more than usual. He knew his son had helped them dispose of the body, and had found out where only a few days ago. He figured that he had to come to the police with the information. He explained he didn't' come forward sooner due to not having any proof of the murder.

Sanders had researched the backgrounds of Cowboy and Brianna. The two looked good for the murder. The young one, Jonathan, seemed to be just a regular college kid that was just pulled into a bad deal. Herman played that angle up as well. Although he wanted Jonathan to pay for his act of disloyalty and disrespect, he didn't want to see him in the same kind of trouble as Cowboy and Brianna. He totally left Charrise out the picture, knowing that he had done enough to her already. Lastly, he was saving Lorraine for himself, but he knew he had to get the others out the way to have a clear path at bringing down his wrath on her.

"Let's go, and remember to move only on my demand. Keep in mind if they draw first, we will take their asses down." Sanders said as he strapped on his bulletproof vest.

Herman winced in pain. He knew he had only a little time to have the surgery done to repair his intestines and pancreas. The pain was getting worse by the day, and the drinking had stopped numbing the pain. The money he had taken from Brianna would more than pay for the surgery, but he needed more for him to go off and start a new pain free life. He could leave now, but the thought of them mother fuckers being here happy was just too much for him. He wanted them gone, either by casket or by gavel.

Cowboy sat in his car watching the motel. Lorraine had given him names of cheap places that were near juke joint bars that Herman liked to go to when he wanted to have a night out. Cowboy had shown his picture to the clerk along with a hundred dollar bill. The clerk told him what room Herman was in and that he had been there a couple of days. Cowboy handed her another hundred and went back outside to his car. He knew that Herman would be leaving his room soon to meet with Brianna. He could not kill Herman at the hotel after the clerk had seen him and knew he was asking about him. He would have to make sure that he took him out swiftly and disposed of his body.

Cowboy studied the door marked with the number 41. He was checking his watch, just as Herman walked out the door. Herman took a drink from a bottle in a brown bag. *This nigga is pathetic. The world will be a better place without him occupying space in it.* Cowboy thought to himself as he exited his car. He checked the .45 automatic to make sure he had the safety off.

Herman began his walk to his vehicle, mumbling to himself and drinking.

Cowboy picked up his pace as Herman got closer to his car. On second thought, he was going to take this fool out right here. Cowboy intensified his pace and raised his gun. He was within ten yards of Herman, when Herman suddenly turned around, and locked eyes on the gun, and then Cowboy. Cowboy took satisfaction in seeing Herman's face before he pulled the trigger. He smiled at Herman and began to squeeze the trigger. Tires squealed and a black minivan pulled up behind Herman's automobile.

"Shit," Cowboy said. The police had shown up, but how?

The door opened and women wearing black bandanas and hoodies jumped out. They had automatic weapons pointing at Herman. One of them hit him with the butt of the gun in the face.

Herman yelled.

"Move nigga!" one of the women yelled as she pushed him towards the van.

The second female looked back at Cowboy standing with his gun drawn and opened fire in his direction. Cowboy ran towards a parked car. He turned and fired back before jumping behind the car as bullets zinged by him.

"Let's go! We don't have time for this!" Cowboy heard one of the females yell.

The bullets stopped and Cowboy waited a few moments before he looked up. He heard the sound of the tires screeching out of the parking lot. He slowly stood, just in time to see the van disappear onto the side street. He put the gun inside his pants and began to walk back towards his car. He opened the door, took a deep breath, and felt a burning sensation in his side. He looked down at his light blue shirt and a red spot was growing on his right side.

"Shit." Cowboy said as she started the sedan. He looked in the backseat and grabbed Lorraine's wrap. He pressed it against the wound and pulled out of the motel parking lot just as the blue lights were approaching.

Chapter 13

Brianna checked her watch. She threw the large duffle bag on her shoulder and began to walk towards the patio of the restaurant. As she sat down at a table, her phone whistled with messages from Jonathan and Kasy, letting her know that they could see her and were nearby. She placed the duffle bag under the table. She did not have anywhere near the million dollars that Herman had demanded in the bag. She twisted the ring on her index finger and checked the streets for any signs of her stepfather. He was ten minutes late. She was beginning to get nervous. She had followed his instructions without flaw.

Brianna began to wonder why he had not shown up yet. He was specific about wanting her to meet him outside. Her street senses kicked in. She knew Herman really didn't care about the money. What he cared about was revenge, and pain. Her paranoia began to get the best of her. She looked around at some of the windows and began to wonder if Herman was in one them with her in cross hairs. She wanted to leave, especially now that it was twenty minutes past the time for him to have his ass there.

"Where the fuck is this nigga?" Brianna mumbled to herself.

"Hello ma'am, my name is Danny. May I get you something to drink?"

Brianna huffed and checked her watch. "Uh yeah, just some water for now."

"Yes ma'am," the waiter said as he placed a coaster on the table.

Detective Sanders sat in the back of the small cargo truck. He watched Brianna on the monitor.

"You should have eyes on one and two now."

"Yeah, yeah subject one is the brother, correct? But did you ID the other person yet?" the officer asked.

"No, the plates go to a Mitzi Jones. We trying to see if he is in our system by face recognition. Where the hell is this Herman guy?" Officer Thompson asked as he poured some coffee.

"I don't know, he's late. I tried his phone but it went straight to voice mail. Send a unit over to that motel; he should be here by now." Detective Sanders said to Officer Thompson.

Thompson nodded and took out his cell phone to send uniforms over to the motel.

Sanders looked at his watch, and then zoomed his camera in on Brianna's face. He could see she was as anxious as they were. She was looking around and biting her lower lip. Something was off, and he could feel it, but all they could do right then was wait.

Brianna's phone vibrated against the table, making her jump. She looked at the screen. Cowboy was calling. She knew he was probably nervous and anxious about the meeting.

"Hey Daddy, I—"

"Baby girl, I got hit, and I am trying to make my way to the hospital." Cowboy said. He was breathing heavily, and Brianna could hear traffic in the background.

"Daddy, what? Where are you? Who shot you?"

"I, I don't know, I..." Cowboy's voice faded, and all Brianna could hear was the sound of cars and the wind in the window.

Cowboy struggled to stay conscious. This wasn't the first time he had been hit with hot lead. He could tell by the color and the amount of blood that the bullet had hit or nicked something major. The road in front of him began to sway back and forth. He shook his head, trying to stay focused.

"Daddy! Daddy!" Brianna yelled into the phone as she grabbed the black duffle bag and slung it back over her shoulder.

Jonathan and Kasy could tell by the pace of her walk that something was wrong, and began running back to their vehicles.

"All subjects are on the move, do we take them down, sir?"

Sanders watched as Brianna bolted across the street.

"Sir, do we take them down?" the officer yelled a second time.

"No, stand down, stand down. Everyone just stand down, do not move!" Sanders said as he made his way to the front of the surveillance truck. "Thompson, follow them, but not too close."

Thompson nodded and started the truck. "What the hell is going on?" Sanders said as Thompson pulled out onto the street.

The officers assigned to Kasy saw him throw his gun in the passenger seat. Instead of standing down, they turned their lights on.

Kasy looked in the rear view mirror and then back at the gun in the seat. "Fuck!" Kasy said. If he was searched and found with a weapon, this would be his third strike.

The engine of his Cobra revved as he looked at the officer in the rear view and the street. He punched the gas and spun out. The officers took off after him. Kasy's car was built for speed, and he was a good driver. The cops had a difficult time maneuvering through the residential streets. Kasy knew he needed to get to the interstate to lose these pigs.

"Detective, they have engaged the unidentified male. He had a gun, and the officers are pursuing him." Thompson said.

"What the fuck did I say? Fuck!" Sanders yelled as he grabbed the CB.

"Who is in pursuit?" Sanders said.

"It is Officers Adams and Smith, sir."

"Did I not say stand down? Where are you idiots?"

"Pursuing the subject on Woodlawn, sir." Officer Smith said as Adams made a sharp turn. The helicopter flew above, giving support to the units on the ground.

Kasy cursed as he missed the exit to I-77. He knew he had to make his way to the next exit, which was I-85 about three miles down the road.

Sanders and Thompson joined the pursuit. "Everyone back off a little... we can't risk hurting civilians! Did you get that, Smith and Adams?"

"Copy," Officer Smith said looking at Adams. "Shit man, I told you to calm down. We are going against orders."

"What was I supposed to do? The guy had a gun." Adams answered while weaving between cars, not wanting to let Kasy out of his sight. This was his first year on the force, and he didn't want to be a uniform cop for long. He needed to prove himself, and if that meant disobeying orders for the greater good, then so be it. "Don't worry I will take the heat for this."

Kasy was just about to cross over West Boulevard when an SUV swerved into his lane, and hit its breaks, causing Kasy to crash into the back of it. He felt another impact to the side of his car, and his leg snapping. There were sounds in the distance of metal hitting metal, and the smell of burning rubber.

"Shit!" Adams said as he grabbed the CB to report the crashes. Units converged on the scene and officers jumped from their cars to check on the people in the vehicles.

The driver of the SUV staggered out of the truck and ran back to check on Kasy. Smith ran up to the mangled Mustang and asked the man to step back.

"Hands outside the car!" Smith yelled. "I said hands outside the car!"

"Smith, the door is jammed. Shit, he might be dead." Adams said as he assisted the woman from the Honda that had slammed into the side of Kasy's car.

"This mutha fucka hears me!" he yelled.

Adams looked on in amazement as Smith climbed over the Honda and pulled back what was left of Kasy's windshield. Kasy had a huge gash in his forehead and his arm was stuck between the door of the car and his seat. Adams gave the woman to the EMT, and trotted back to the Mustang.

Smith had his gun drawn on Kasy, who seemed barely conscious.

"I said, hands up." Smith yelled again.

"Smith! Smith the man can't move." Adams spoke, trying to bring some reasoning to his partner. He then reached in through the window and grabbed the .45 from the floor. "I need a medic over here now." Adams yelled.

Sanders ran up to the car, and looked in. "What the ... damn!" Sanders said, looking at the blood oozing from Kasy's forehead. Sanders kicked the Honda, and then looked up at Smith who had his gun drawn on Kasy. Before Thompson could stop him, Sanders was on the hood of the Mustang punching Smith.

Officers rushed to separate the two men as the fireman and EMT yelled for them to get back. They were going to have to use the Jaws of Life to get Kasy out of the car. Thompson finally got Sanders to let go of Smith and dragged his partner back to the police truck.

"Detective, you need to calm down!" Thompson said, pushing him inside the truck.

"Stupid, stupid, stupid!" Sanders yelled as he sat down in the seat. "What a mess!"

Chapter 14

Herman slowly opened his eyes; a strong smell of feces hit his nose. He tried to move, but realized that his hands and feet had been bound to a chair. The gag in his mouth tasted sour and smelled like shit. He had to fight back the vomit that was making its way up his throat. He could only see light through the black cloth bag that covered his head. Mixed with the smell of shit, was the smell of marijuana. He wished he could have put his teeth between the rag and his tongue, but the gag had been tied tightly and he couldn't prevent tasting the rancid cloth.

Selena sat in a chair in front of Herman blowing smoke from her blunt into his face. She took one last hit off the Backwoods and stood. She snatched the bag off his head. Herman blinked to adjust his eyes to the light. Once he could focus, his stomach dropped as he looked into Selena's cold glare. Her anger and pain smoldered in her eyes. Seeing the daggers fly from her fierce look, Herman knew that his pleas for mercy would fall on deaf ears.

"So nigga, you comfy?" Selena asked as she stood. "I hope so, how do you like this place huh? Lovely isn't it?" She inhaled, laughed, and took out a piece of gum. "Man, I had a nasty taste in my mouth. But nothing like the taste you have in your mouth, huh? Yeah I wanted to find something that was similar to the bad taste I had, and still have in my mouth from what you did to my baby cousin. I know no matter how much I brush, gargle, and hell, get cleanings I still will never get that taste out my mouth. So I want to make sure that you shared in my experience. The closest thing I could find to match the taste in my mouth from that night was some dog shit." Selena said, pointing to the gag in Herman's mouth.

Herman began struggling, and let out a muffled yell at Selena. She shook her head as she walked over to the window. The females who had snatched Herman for her sat on the steps talking, texting, and laughing. Selena watched them. They had shown her loyalty and love in her time of need. They had proven they would ride with her by kidnapping Herman's ass for her, and now they were waiting to do whatever they needed to do to help her get her revenge.

"Yeah nigga, I mean bitch, cause you are definitely not a man! What kind of man would allow his daughter to be kidnapped, raped, and then kill an unarmed child?" Selena yelled.

Herman looked at her with terror in his eyes.

Selena flexed her hand and laid an upper cut across Herman's jaw, knocking him and the chair back.

The women ran in the house, hearing the commotion. "You okay," Ivory said looking at Herman laying on the floor.

"Yeah, I'm great. Help me get this piece of shit up." Selena said to Ivory.

Ivory and Selena lifted the chair up. She flexed her right hand and smiled at Herman. He coughed, and blood from the missing tooth and his cut tongue spewed on his shirt.

Selena looked at him. He was slumped over, coughing and in pain. For a moment, she had pity on him, then her mind went to seeing Chatima lying on the floor in a pool of blood and the sounds of her aunt's voice screaming when she called to give her the news. No, it would be no pity in her heart for this nigga.

Selena bent down close to Herman's ear. "You ready to die, motherfucker?" Selena yelled at him, as she punched him again in the cheek, and then spit in his face. The spit landed on his forehead and slid down his nose. She pulled out her glock and placed the barrel between his eyes. "Nah, nigga… a quick death is too good for a motherfucker like you." Her finger felt numb as she held it on the trigger, so she took a deep breath and sat down in the chair that was in front of Him.

"Ummmm... ummmm... ummmmm." Herman kept trying to speak with the gag in his mouth. Selena reached down and pulled the rag out his mouth temporarily. She wanted to hear his last pleas for life.

"Say your piece, nigga, before I send you to hell."

With a quaking voice, he mustered out a sentence. "Let me say something before you kill me," Herman pleaded. "Trust me, I think you want to hear this. If you kill me right now, Brianna and Charrise's mother won't live to see next week. Starvation and dehydration will claim her life in the most vicious way," Herman said, turning his head to spit out a glob of blood.

Selena felt a chill go up her back. She studied Herman; hearing him mention harm coming to Lorraine caused her finger to squeeze the trigger. She steadied herself for a moment, this was just one of his bullshit attempts to weasel his way out of paying his debt for what he had done. However, she needed to be sure that he was only bluffing. She pressed the barrel of the gun against his forehead again.

"Nigga what you talking about?"

"I got her somewhere safe... for now," he answered, giving Selena a serious look.

"You lyin'," she shot back.

"Try to call her then… Call that bitch Brianna or Charrise, I guarantee you they haven't heard nothing from her." Herman said, now starting to smile.

Selena got up, walked over to her purse sitting on the table and retrieved her cell phone from it. She punched in Lorraine's cell phone number and it went straight to voicemail. She quickly hung up the phone and then tried to call the house phone. That line just kept ringing and ringing. Lorraine was not answering, and with each ring, Selena's heart rate increased. She looked at Herman sitting in the chair. She had to stop herself from screaming and unloading the clip into him. Her head began to spin, so she braced herself against the wall.

Brianna and Jonathan pulled up to Charlotte Memorial Hospital, only to see Cowboy's car surrounded by police officers and detectives in front of the emergency room door. Brianna's heart raced after seeing blood all over his steering wheel and driver's seat. The detectives were trying to take as many pictures and collect as much evidence as they could before they placed the car on the flatbed. Brianna and Jonathan hurried into the emergency room lobby and walked up to the admissions station.

"I'm looking for my father. His name is Mr. Parson," she said, walking up to the nurses' station.

The nurse keyed something into the computer. She slid her finger down the screen. "Your father has been taken into surgery. I can have someone take you to the waiting area."

"How was he when they brought him in?" Brianna asked, fighting back tears.

"He drove himself here, Ms. Parson. When he got inside, he collapsed, and we rushed him to the OR. I'm sorry that is all the information I have right now."

Jonathan wrapped his arms around Brianna and led her to a chair. She buried her face in his shoulder and cried. She began to pray to God, begging him not to take her father away from her.

Charrise needed some time to herself, away from everyone. The last year and half had really taken a toll on her. She had gone from being totally in love with Dre, to being raped and finding out that her own father was partially or maybe even totally responsible. She would never truly know, since it was evident that Brianna and everyone else was keeping secrets from her. Charrise shook her head, hoping to get those and other memories out her mind. *Not today,* she thought to herself. Although she had checked into Ballantine resort and spa two days ago, she had spent the full 48 hours inside her room, soaking and crying. But today, she had made up her mind that she would enjoy the amenities available to her.

She took her time going through the brochure of the resort to see what activities would suit her best. She decided on the "Golf for the Day" package. Although she couldn't play a lick of golf, she knew she felt like hitting something. She needed to release some stress, and maybe that little white ball would do the trick. The golf package started with a gourmet breakfast. Once Charrise looked over at the clock, she realized that the morning meal would be served in less than twenty minutes. She knew she didn't have time for a full shower, so she would have to settle with a quick wash up.

She sat her naked body on the side of the tub, and with the water running, cleaned her key areas. She quickly brushed her teeth and slipped on her white True Religion shorts and a red and white Polo golf shirt. The only shoes she had were sandals, so she knew she would need to purchase some golf shoes from the lobby store. She was going to have to buy a hat also, because it would take at least another hour to get her hair straight. It was times like these that she envied Brianna and Selena, with their long good Indian hair. The thought of her two girls made her smile. She knew that both loved her tremendously and would do anything for her. But she was tired of them and everyone else treating her like a child when it was convenient for them. She knew she would have to forgive them at some point, but as of right now, she was going to make them suffer before she did so.

Walking into the downstairs reception area, Charrise really took in the beautiful decor of the resort. The weather was perfect to be outside, so she took a table on the outdoor patio. While in the resort store, she had picked up a pair of Gucci frame sunglasses while purchasing her golf shoes and hat. The shades were quite expensive, but she was using the credit card that Brianna had given her for expenditures when she traveled for business.

Shit, she owes me. Charrise thought to herself before placing the glasses and the other items on the counter.

"Hey you... I hate to be staring at you like I was, but I'm sure I have met you, I just can't seem to place where, and it's bothering me tremendously."

Charrise snapped out of her daze. She looked at the nice looking white man with confusion. She was so into her thoughts she hadn't noticed anyone looking in her direction. She was almost sure he didn't know her, nor her him. Then as she looked closer, it was something very familiar about the gentleman; she just couldn't figure out what.

"Well, do you mind if I join you for breakfast and maybe we can figure it out together?" the man asked

Now, Charrise was not sure if this was just a great pickup line, or if they did indeed know each other. *If it is a pickup line, it was a very unique one,* she thought. *He is nice looking though, and I am a little lonely.* She continued to reason with herself.

"Sure, why not." she responded with a smile. The man sat down and they began talking like old classmates who were catching up after years of not seeing each other. After chatting about where they were from, the subject of occupation came up. Charrise, unsure of what profession to claim, insisted that Alston go first.

"Well, if you must know, I'm a Doctor, a gynecologist to be exact. I work at Caroline Health Care."

Alston didn't have to finish his statement, before Charrise realized where they had seen each other. He was the fine doctor who had called for the woman who went before her at the clinic. All kind of thoughts began to run through her mind. The first and most important being whether or not he knew why she was there that day. Alston was still talking about his career, so it seemed that, unlike Charrise, he had not put his work and seeing her together yet. *He probably sees hundreds of women in any given week. It's no way he will make that connection, even so, I could have been there for a simple checkup or anything.* Charrise thought to herself.

"Ok, enough about my work, what type of work do you do?" Alston asked with a raised brow.

"Actually, I'm a fulltime student and I sell Herbalife products part-time." Charrise responded.

"Well you must do very well with your health products to be able to spend a weekend at a resort like this." Alston replied.

"I do pretty well, and I'm spending a week, not a weekend." Charrise uttered. It was her way of letting

Alston know that she wasn't a female in need of a come up, and she could handle herself financially.

Alston and Charrise enjoyed each other's company for all eighteen holes of the golf course. While Alston started off serious, by the fourth hole, he was only interested in helping Charrise with her form. So that meant being close enough to smell her wonderful scent and feel her still thick curvy figure against his body.

Both were sweating profusely and Charrise was about to invite him up to her room, so they could shower and make dinner plans, when her phone began to ring. It was Selena. She had not talked to her girl in a while, so she decided to answer.

The doctor entered the waiting room. Brianna and Jonathan had been there for nearly six hours. Brianna refused to go home until she saw her father.

"Ms. Parsons?" the tall slim doctor said as he looked at Brianna. "My name is Dr. Morris. I am your father's surgeon." Dr. Morris said, extending his hand to Brianna.

"It's Campbell. How is my dad?"

"Well, Ms. Campbell, it was touch and go. He has lost a lot of blood, and we had to remove some of his intestines. The bullet went straight through him. He is resting now. You can see him for a few minutes, but he is still heavily sedated."

"Thank you, Doctor," Brianna said holding Jonathan's hand.

They followed the doctor through the double doors. The fluorescent lights seemed to become brighter as they approached the ICU. Brianna could smell the disinfectants and hear the machines monitoring patients. Dr. Morris stopped at room six.

"Only one of you can go in, and only for a few moments."

Brianna squeezed Jonathan's hand and opened the door. Cowboy lay in the bed with tubes, and wires coming out of him. Brianna touched his hand and sat down on the stool beside the bed.

"Daddy." Brianna kissed his hand and laid her head on the bed beside his arm. "You get better, Daddy, cause I need you." Brianna wiped her eyes and kissed his forehead.

The machines beeped as she watched his chest rise and fall. "I'm gonna find out who did this, and take their fucking head off." She squeezed his hand and then pulled the covers up on him. She looked back at him one last time before leaving the room.

"I love you, Daddy," she said before closing the door.

"How is he?" a man said, practically running into Brianna. Brianna recognized him from the courthouse. It was Cowboy's son... well, her brother.

"He is resting right now. He is really sedated." Brianna said.

"I want to see him." Eagle said, walking past her into the room.

Brianna looked at Jonathan, and sat down beside him.

"Hey sis, I don't know Cowboy that well, but from what I can tell he is one tough dude. He is going to be all right. That guy is a beast. He probably gonna wake up and smoke a cigarette in the ICU." Jonathan said, laughing.

"Yeah, he probably will. He is tough, a real O.G.." Brianna said, wiping her nose with a tissue.

They sat there silently for a few moments. Brianna's phone rang. She looked at the screen and saw Charrise's picture. She hit ignore; she did not want to deal with Charrise right now. Right now, she just wanted to concentrate on her father. She scrolled through her contact list and dialed her mother's number. Lorraine's voicemail picked up without even ringing. She called again and the voicemail picked up again.

"Ma, where are you? I need you to come to the hospital. Cowboy has been shot." Brianna pressed end and sat back in the chair. It was not like her mother not to answer her phone, but it was like her not to charge her phone. Brianna decided to text her as well. She knew she would see the text as soon as she turned on her phone. Her phone buzzed. She looked at the screen, Charrise was calling her again, she was about to hit ignore for the second time, but paused.

"Yeah?" Brianna said with an attitude that Charrise could feel through the phone.

"Why yo ass send me to voice mail?" Charrise said, sitting in the car watching the cops watch her parents' house.

"What do you want?" Brianna said, looking at her nails.

"Where is Ma? Is she with you?"

"No, she isn't with me. I'm at the hospital. Cowboy got shot. I just tried calling her and she didn't answer. Why?" Brianna asked nonchalantly.

"He got shot by who?"

"I don't know, Charrise, he just got out of surgery."

"Was Ma with him?" Charrise asked, feeling her pulse quicken.

"I just said that I tried calling her, Charrise. No, she wasn't with him. Look, what's up?" The line was quiet for a moment. "Charrise! What is wrong? Why are you asking about Ma? I am sure she is fine."

"Herman says that she isn't fine, and I can't reach her." Charrise said, putting her keys in the ignition.

"Herman? Where did you see him?" Brianna said, standing.

"That doesn't matter, I need to find Ma." Charrise said trying to hide the panic she was feeling.

"Charrise, where did you see Herman?"

"I don't have time to talk about Herman now. I need to find my mother."

"Charrise, what is going on? Where are you?" Brianna said, raising her voice slightly.

"I am about to handle some shit you should have handled months ago." Charrise said.

Brianna heard a click and then silence.

"Was that Charrise?" Jonathan asked.

Brianna shook her head and walked over to the window of the waiting room. The sun had gone down. She checked her watch; it was almost seven. She dialed her mother's number again, and Lorraine's voice mailed picked up.

"Jonathan, have your heard from Mommy today?" she asked.

"No." Jonathan said, taking out his phone. He had not checked his phone all day. He saw a few text messages from people, but one caught his eye. A message from Gator was sent earlier that day.

"Did she call you?" Brianna asked as she dialed Lorraine's number again.

Jonathan shook his head.

"Something is up." Brianna said, walking around the room.

She took her phone out and called Kasy. His phone rang several times and went to voicemail. Brianna wondered why he wasn't answering, and why he had not followed them to the hospital.

Brianna felt a twinge in her stomach, making her sit down for a moment. She inhaled.

The door to Cowboy's room opened and Eagle walked out. He walked over to Brianna and touched her shoulder. "Hey, you okay?" he asked as he sat down beside her. "Pops is strong, he is going to pull through." Eagle said, wrapping his arms around Brianna's shoulder.

"I hope so, Eagle." She looked up to see the police walking into the waiting area.

“Here come these mutherfuckas.” Eagle whispered.

“Ms. Campbell? My name is Detective Sanders,” the white detective said, showing her his badge. “The doctor says your father is lucky to be alive. Any idea who would have shot him?”

“If we knew that, do you think we would be sitting here?” Eagle said without looking at the detective.

“And you are?” Detective Sanders said, looking Eagle over.

“I am trying to comfort my sister while our father fights for his life. So why don’t you get your ass out there and pretend to look for who put him in that fucking bed!” Eagle said as he stood.

He pulled Brianna up and motioned for Jonathan to follow him. They exited the waiting room and walked outside. Eagle didn’t say anything as he walked to his white Range Rover. He opened the door for Brianna, as Jonathan got in the back seat.

“I can’t stand them muthafuckas.” he said as he drove out of the parking lot. “You guys hungry? Because I’m starving, let’s get something to eat. The doctors have my number if something changes with Pops. In the meantime, we need to find out what the hell happened to him.”

Chapter 15

Selena and Charrise sat in the parked minivan in the front yard of the house. Charrise had rushed to the address once Selena called and told her what Herman had done to their mother. She tried to get as much info as possible from Brianna, but it was like she was bothering her, so she never let her know Lorraine was in danger. Charrise figured she would handle it herself.

Herman was doubled over, tired from the beating that Selena and the rest of the girls had given him. Selena tossed a cup of soda in Herman's face to wake him up.

Herman smiled at her, and laughed when he saw Charrise sitting there beside her.

"No luck, huh?" he said as he coughed. "You just wasted valuable time, girl. I told you I am the one that will decide if Lorraine lives or dies. It all depends on what you and that bitch Brianna do. Hey baby girl, I see they done dragged you into this now."

"Don't fuckin call me that!" Charrise said, trying to fight back tears. "Why are you doing this to me? I am your flesh and blood, and she is your wife. Why are you so heartless?" Charrise said looking into Herman's eyes. Herman laughed at her.

As he laughed, he began to cough. The taste of the shitty rag lingered on his tongue

"You really are sick. How do you do shit like this to your own flesh and blood? How you allow your child to be tortured and raped?" Charrise asked with tears forming in her eyes.

"They told you that? That little red hoe promised that she wouldn't—"

"So you don't deny it, do you asshole?" Charrise responded cutting Herman off. She didn't want to hear any more of his lies, so she picked the rag up off the floor and stuck it back into his mouth.

Charrise walked back to the chair and sat down. She stared at Herman, thinking of her childhood. Unlike Brianna, he had always showered her with affection and love. He never mistreated her and was always supportive of her in every way. She wondered would she be able to kill him to save her mother. She wished Brianna was there to take the decision out her hands.

Brianna, and Jonathan sat at the table with Eagle. Jonathan took out his phone and texted Gator, hoping that she was not pissed off at him for responding to her so late.

"The cops have Pop's car, but I have a friend at the station that was able to get me the GPS information.

I know where he was before he went to the hospital." Eagle said, sipping his coffee.

Brianna stared at her half-brother. Eagle had high cheekbones, smooth caramel skin, and large brown eyes that seemed to change with his mood. At six foot two, broad shoulders, he had the build of a running back. As handsome as he was, he seemed to be just as dangerous as Cowboy.

"Brianna, you need to eat, cause we got a lot of work ahead of us. Now what was your sister saying about your mother?" Eagle said, taking a bite of his burger.

"I don't know. She asked where she was, and then said Herman said she was in danger. She wouldn't give me any more details." Brianna answered.

"What do you mean Charrise said, he said, Mom was in danger?" Jonathan asked, putting his phone down.

"That is what she told me, and then she hung up. I asked her where she was, and she said taking care of something I should have taken care of months ago."

Jonathan picked up his phone and dialed Charrise's number. He needed to get this shit straight, especially when it was dealing with his mom. The phone rang several times before going to voicemail.

Eagle dug into his pocket and pulled out a wad of cash. He took three twenties from the knot and placed them on the table.

"Come on, we need to go to that hotel," Eagle said, walking towards the door. Brianna and Jonathan followed him. Jonathan's phone chirped, making him smile at the text message.

I do not do well with being put off. Jonathan stared at the screen. Even with the shit going on, Jonathan could not get Gator off his mind. He had to be smart about what he would say to her. He slowed his pace and let Eagle and Brianna walk ahead of him. Jonathan dialed Gator's number. The phone rang a few times, and Jonathan thought it was going to go to voice mail.

"Hello." Gator said.

"Hello beautiful, beautiful lady. I wanted to call to apologize to you. Things have been a little crazy. I promise you, I will make this up to you." Jonathan said. The line was silent for a moment.

"I'm glad you called me, Jonathan. I was actually worried about you." Gator said. "Where are you right now?"

"I'm with my sister and her brother. We got to go handle some business." Jonathan said.

"Business, like the business you handled in the parking lot of the condo or the business your friend handled on Betty Ford?" Gator said.

Jonathan stopped walking. He didn't even notice that Eagle and Brianna were already in the truck.

"It could be both, babe."

"Sounds good to me, papi. Just be careful, okay." Gator said before hanging up.

"Jonathan, let's go!" Brianna yelled from the vehicle.

Jonathan began walking towards the SUV. He wanted to call Gator back, but Brianna and Eagle were telling him to get in the truck.

"What were you doing dude?" Brianna asked.

"Just handling some business, sis. Sorry."

Brianna's phone vibrated. She looked down at the screen and could see it was Brandon again. She pressed ignore and looked out the window. It was early evening now, but the sun had not gone down. It seemed like shit was always happening. There was never a moment's peace. Her mind drifted back to Tre, and how he had made her feel so safe. He had protected and shielded her from so much shit. Even with her now being with Brandon, he could not make her feel as secure and protected, as she always felt with Tre. Tre's reputation in the streets was feared, and respected. The only thing Brianna had to worry about or so she thought, was what trip they were going to take, and the color of her next Hermes bag.

She wished he was here now, because Herman wouldn't have dared cross her. Tre would have planted a piece of lead between his eyes just based on the way he had treated Brianna during her childhood.

Eagle pulled into the parking lot of a small motel off Graham Street. He parked in front of the office, took out his phone and made a call.

"We outside." he said and then hung up the phone.

A few minutes later, a petite woman walked towards the SUV. She had her hair pulled back in a ponytail. She wore a white baby tee and khaki capris that seemed to be two sizes too small. She opened the back door of the truck.

“Hey,” she said nearly out of breath. “How y’all doing?” Brianna and Jonathan spoke to her, but Eagle cut straight to the point.

“Aight, so what you see today?” Eagle said turning around to look at her.

“Well, I saw these chicks pull up in a gray minivan. They jumped out with ski masks and shit on they face. They grabbed old dude, and threw him in the van, and then started firing shots. I saw a man running to get behind some cars. These fools was popping it off like dey was in fucking Afghanistan!” the woman said laughing.

“A gray minivan? Did you see who was driving it?” Jonathan asked, thinking back to his house being shot up.

“No, I couldn’t see shit but dem bullets flying every damn where.”

“So did you tell the cops this?” Eagle asked as he opened the glove compartment.

“You know what, dem fools ain’t even asked me nothing yet. You’d think that they would have, just goes to show you how our tax dollars work. I bet if this shit was in Ballantine they would have pulled every mug in this joint.” Teela said laughing.

“Well, if they do get around to asking you bout what you saw.” Eagle said, handing her an envelope. “You hid under the counter when you heard the shots.”

Teela took the envelope and opened it. “Yeah... gotcha.” Teela said.

Eagle nodded to her and she opened the door. She practically sprinted back inside.

"Gray minivan? That is what those bitches were driving that shot up the house, Bri." Jonathan said. "Fuck, why would they shoot Cowboy and take Herman?" Jonathan asked.

"They shot up your house? Why?" Eagle asked, looking at Jonathan.

Jonathan looked out the window. He did not want to discuss what he and his crew had done. Trying to find out what was going on with the Cowboy situation had taken his mind off his fallen friends, and now they seemed connected.

"Jonathan!" Brianna said.

"What Bri? Fuck! I robbed some bitches, okay. They shot Kevin and I took out one of theirs." Jonathan rubbed his hands over his face.

Eagle shook his head and looked at Brianna.

"Nigga, who you fuck with?" Eagle asked irritated. In the back of his mind he knew that there was only one set of females that would be worth robbing in the QC, and who were organized enough to take retribution.

"Some bitches that run Betty Ford Road." Jonathan said.

"You fucked with the wrong crew, brah." Eagle said.

He thought about Niya being locked up for three years. He knew that this young fool had robbed and murdered one of her crew. He looked at his sister, and then Jonathan. This young boy had no idea what he had done, and Eagle wasn't sure how he was going to help fix the situation. Gwen was running shit while Niya was away. Ever since the shit with her son, she seemed to have gone into straight goon mode. Shit had just gotten deeper and real.

Chapter 16

Herman's back and his stomach were on fire. The pain had gone from throbbing to shooting. He had to mask his ache in front of Charrise and Selena, but when they left to go outside, he took the opportunity to attempt to adjust himself in the chair. His hands had gone numb from being tied behind his back, and each breath he took seemed to set his chest on fire. He knew that a couple of ribs were broken by the pain in his right side.

"All right Herman..." Charrise said as she entered the room. "What do you want? What do I need to do to save my mother?"

"Well the more you play around, the longer she will suffer. Kill Brianna, let me go and save your mama or kill me and let her die all alone."

Charrise wanted to blow Herman's brains out, but the thought of her mother suffering stopped her. This nigga was really crazy; he had really gone off the deep end. She knew that his hatred of her sister and her mother would carry him through any torture she could dish out.

Gator checked her text messages. Jonathan was blowing up her phone with questions about where she was and when she was coming back. Maybe she was going to have to lay off giving him that good-good for a while, because he was damn near in stalker mode. She wanted to make sure she had him on a string, but just not following her around on the other end of it. The product Jonathan had been robbing these bitches for had proved to be great quality, and tonight she was putting the finishing touches on her deal. Gator was glad that Moon decided to wear a dress, make up and stilettos this evening. She thought that Moon only owned jeans and Nike shoes.

When she stepped out in a Prada cocktail dress that hugged the curves she always hid, wearing pink Prada open toe shoes with matching purse, and her dreads pinned in a beautiful bun on top of her head, with pink shingle earrings, Gator gasped.

"I can clean it up when I have to, "Moon told Gator with a smile as she hit the switch on the gate.

"May I help you?" a voice with a thick accent said through the speaker.

"Yes, this is Gator. We are expected."

The large iron gate opened. Moon drove through, looking over the grounds. There were large Magnolia trees that lined the driveway, giving the drive a true *Gone with the Wind* feel. They pulled up to the large mansion and a young man opened Moon's door. He extended his hand to help her down, and took the keys. He ran to the other passenger side and opened the door for Gator.

Gator smiled at him and stepped down. She reached back in and grabbed the large black tote bag. Gator and Moon walked up to the door and walked inside. Music filled the foyer, and the house. They looked around at the people dancing and drinking.

A tall blonde walked by, eyeing Moon up and down. Moon and Gator looked at each other and laughed. Moon grabbed a glass of champagne from one of the servers walking by, and sipped it.

"Damn, Gate, this the good shit." she whispered to Gator.

"Gator, you look delicious!" Gaston said as he kissed her cheek. He twirled her around, and scanned her. She wore a turquoise Gucci sheer blouse with white pants, and gold strappy Gucci sandals. "And who is this?" Gaston said, turning to Moon.

"This is Moon." Gator said.

Gaston took Moon's hand and kissed it. "Moon, how are you? Glad you could join us."

Moon smiled at him, and slowly slipped her hand from his grip. "Well ladies, let's go upstairs to my office." Gaston motioned towards the stairs.

Gator and Moon began to ascend the stairs behind him. Moon made a mental note of the two men standing outside the doors of the office. They were large and concealed some serious heat. Gaston pointed to the two large leather chairs in front of his desk. He took off his sports coat and hung it on the back of his chair.

"Would you like something to drink?" Gaston said as he poured scotch into a glass.

"No thank you, Gaston. So your text said to come to this party, are you interested in our product?" Gator asked.

"Interested?" Gaston said laughing. "I am more than interested." Gaston opened the drawer of his desk and pulled out a large gold envelope.

Moon smiled and leaned forward to take the packet. She opened it, and nodded to Gator.

Gator smiled at Gaston then she stood and opened the large tote bag. She placed five bricks of raw coke on his desk. Gaston placed the bricks back into the bag and closed it. Both women stood to depart.

"Ladies I know you are not going to leave. Please stay and enjoy the party. Mingle, I insist."

Gator smiled at him and nodded.

Eagle pulled back up to the front of the hospital. Brianna and Jonathan got out. Jonathan began to walk through the sliding doors, and Brianna stopped.

"Jonathan, we have to talk." Brianna said pointing to the metal bench outside the doors. Jonathan turned and sat down beside her. "What the hell is going on? Why would you be robbing anyone? You are supposed to be in school making something of yourself."

"I plan on going back to school, Bri. I just... I mean, look, I can't explain it, okay?" Jonathan said trying to find the words to explain his actions to his sister.

"If you needed money, you know you could have come to me for it." Brianna said, touching his shoulder. Brianna's phone rang. It was Charrise calling again.

"Yeah," Brianna said mouthing Charrise's name to Jonathan.

Eagle had parked the car and was walking up as Brianna put the phone on speaker.

"Look, we got a problem," Charrise said. "Herman has done something with Mommy, and he will not talk to anyone, but you. He says you have something that belongs to him, and you need to bring it to him."

"Where you at?" Brianna asked, looking at Eagle.

"I am at the house off Central." Charrise answered.

Brianna felt her heart stop beating and a chill ran down her spine. "What are you ..."

"Look," Charrise said, cutting her off. "Whatever you got that he wants bring it or our mother will die!" The line clicked and the screen went black. Brianna put the phone in her pocket.

Jonathan rested his face in his hands, and sighed. "What the hell is up with her ass?" Jonathan said, running his hand over his face.

"Something ain't right." Eagle added. "Give me some time to check some things out, Brianna."

"No, you heard what she said. Herman is going to hurt my mother. I can't let that happen." Brianna said, walking towards the parking deck.

Jonathan and Eagle followed her.

“Brianna, something don’t feel right about this. Look, we gotta be smart. What if the nigga is using your sister to draw you out to him?” Eagle said, grabbing her arm.

“Look, I don’t have time for planning. Herman is crazy, and there is no telling what he has done or is going to do to my mother.”

“Where is this place off Central?” Eagle asked.

Brianna reached in her center console and drew a map of the street.

Eagle took the paper. “Brianna, be careful, I don’t like this.” Eagle said again.

Brianna nodded and drove towards the exit of the parking garage.

Jonathan felt the hairs on the back of his neck stand up. Like Eagle, he felt that something about this wasn’t right. Why would Charrise need to meet Brianna at the house off Central? Central Avenue was a rundown, dilapidated area, someone could get killed there and no one would know for weeks. He didn’t think that Charrise would put Brianna in a dangerous situation purposely, but it was a lot going on that he knew he was unaware of.

Brianna drove in silence as Jonathan took out his phone to check his text messages.

“We should probably have someone there in case Cowboy wakes up. Where is Kasy?” Jonathan said realizing that he had not seen Kasy since they left the spot they were supposed to meet Herman.

"I don't know. I tried his phone, and he didn't answer." Brianna responded while keeping her eyes on the road.

Jonathan tried calling Kasy and a woman answered the phone.

"Hello? Who is this?" Jonathan asked.

"This is Detective Johnson. Who am I speaking with?" Jonathan checked the screen to ensure he had dialed the right number.

"Where is Kasy?" Jonathan asked, more annoyed now, realizing he was speaking to a police officer.

"He is in the hospital. Listen, are you a relative of his? If so, you might want to make your way down here," the detective suggested.

"Hospital, what happened?"

"If you could come down, sir, we can explain everything to you."

Jonathan hit end on the screen.

"Fuck, Kasy is in the hospital, the cops said that someone probably needs to get down there." Jonathan said, hitting the dashboard as Brianna turned down Hawthorne.

"Damn, can this day get any more fucked up? Call Damon and Sharon. Tell them to go to the hospital. I want one with my dad and one checking on Kasy." Brianna instructed.

Lorraine's hands were cramping from her using the curved piece of metal to pry the lock off the door. She finally could see a light shining through the hole she had made. Her neck was throbbing from Herman punching her in it from behind. She was glad that he was too drunk to tie the zip ties correctly. It had taken her more than an hour to get them off her wrist. They had sliced her skin as she struggled to slide them down her hand.

Herman was the epitome of evil. He enjoyed inflicting pain on her, but she had stayed with him for her children. Now, he was the biggest threat to their lives. She could finally get the lock off the door, her hands were sore and bloody, but she manage to turn the dead bolt on door, and it finally opened. She ran out into the warehouse, slipped on some oil and twisted her ankle.

"Oh God!" Lorraine screamed. She wanted to sit there and cry, but she knew she had to get to her babies. "Please, Jesus, help me." Lorraine prayed as she tried to stand.

She hobbled over towards the door of the warehouse to find it locked. "No, no!" Lorraine yelled as she beat on the door.

She looked around the warehouse and took a deep breath. She had made it out of the basement, and now she was going to make it outside this damn warehouse, or die trying.

Brianna pulled up to the abandoned looking house on Central Avenue. She scanned the yard, but only saw a van parked in the grass. She and Jonathan got out. Jonathan had his 10mm by his side. He looked at the minivan, trying to make out the color, but it the darkness of the night made it too hard to see. He looked closely at the passenger side of the vehicle. He saw the bullet holes and it confirmed, what he was already thinking. This was the same van that was involved in the shooting at his house and in the killing of A.J. He gripped his gun and followed Brianna up the stairs. There was only one light on in the house.

The door opened and Charrise glared at Brianna.

Brianna walked into the house looking around the living room. She noticed blood on the floor, and a bloody rag. She locked eyes with Charrise and Selena. For some reason, it seemed like the temperature in the room dropped as the ladies stared at each other. So much had happened in the last couple of days, that they really needed to sit down and get things ironed out. But life wouldn't seem to slow down long enough for the words to be said.

Ivory appeared out of the dark kitchen with Herman. Their appearance startled Brianna and she raised her gun.

Herman smiled at her.

"Where is our mother? You sick fuck!" Brianna said taking a step towards him. Herman ignored her and looked at Jonathan.

"Hey son, so it looks like this red bitch done brought you into to this shit as well." Herman said laughing.

"I'm not going to ask you again, Herman." Brianna said as she took another step towards him.

She stopped in her tracks when she saw Ivory click back the chamber of her .45 magnum and point it in her and Jonathan's direction.

Both Selena and Charrise looked at her like she was crazy.

"What are doing Ivory? That's my sister and brother." Charrise yelled while looking at Selena for backup with her statement.

"Yeah, what's going on, Ivory? These our people right here?" Selena chimed in.

"Sorry ladies, but family or no family... This the nigga that killed my sister and the bitch that ordered it!" she said as she kept her gun fastened in their direction.

"Now, how about you put that gun down before we be planning a double funeral! " Ivory instructed seeing the gun Jonathan still had at his side.

"Na fuck that, I ain't putting shit down." Jonathan screamed back, waiting for the opportunity to catch Ivory slipping so he could get a shot off.

"Jonathan just put the gun down. This is obviously some type of misunderstanding, because I haven't had anyone killed. The only person here that I'm interested in seeing dead is this sick old drunk mother fucker right here." Brianna uttered in Herman's direction.

"You better listen to your sister and put that shit down." Ivory said, pulling her other .45 out her back pocket.

"Fuck you bitch, I don't know you!" Jonathan said not taking his eyes off her.

Herman's pulse quickened and he could not stop the smile that spread across his face. All three of the children he raised could be wiped off the face of the earth in a matter of minutes. His cheating ass wife would die from starvation and dehydration, and that motherfucker Cowboy would be put in a cage for the rest of his life. Taking them all down would be worth him taking a bullet. Just as long as none of these mother fuckers breathe free air.

"I'm the bitch that is going to open your skull with a fuckin bullet if you don't put that gun down." Ivory yelled again.

Lorraine managed to crawl through the window of the warehouse. Once she was outside, she sighed, recognizing the familiar street. She knew she was only a few minutes away from the Snapper's restaurant. She had no idea what time it was, but she knew that she could get to a phone there. She ran up the street, her feet were being cut by glass and rocks, but she kept running.

She finally reached the doors of the restaurant and ran inside. Two servers, Sheila and April, were wiping down tables. They stopped and stared at Lorraine who ran past them to the phone at the bar. She fell onto the bar stool and grabbed the phone. Her hands were shaking so badly that she dropped the receiver twice.

"Ugggg!" Lorraine yelled as she snatched the handset from the floor.

"Ms., can I help you? Oh my God, are you ok?" One of the bartenders asked, noticing her wounds.

"Thank you, but I'm fine. I just need to use your phone"

"Ms., you're bleeding." the bartender said, noticing the dried and fresh blood on her arms.

"Ma'am! I'm fine, I just need to use the damn phone!" Lorraine screamed causing her to jump back behind the bar. Lorraine took a deep breath and dialed Cowboy's number. The phone did not ring; it went straight to voicemail, causing Lorraine's heart to stop. "Oh God!" Lorraine said aloud, thinking Herman had accomplished his goal in having Cowboy murdered or locked up.

She sat back in the chair; she needed to gather her thoughts. She took a deep breath and dialed Charrise's number.

Charrise, Jonathan, Brianna, Selena and Ivory had not moved. Each had yelled at the other, and kept their guns locked on one another. The sound of a phone ringing seemed to be miles away. Charrise realized that it was her phone and she pulled it out of her back pocket.

"Hello."

"Charrise?! Thank God you answered! Look, baby, please. Herman is trying to kill Brianna and Cowboy." Lorraine said breathless.

Charrise was relieved to hear her mother's voice. She looked at Brianna with a huge smile.

"So, you are okay? Where are you?" Charrise asked

"Yes, that psycho kidnapped me and locked me in a warehouse, but I escaped. I'm at a restaurant off highway 49. But baby, that's not important. I'll be all right. You need to get to your sister and warn her and Cowboy. That man is crazy, and I'm scared for my baby." Lorraine's voice rose hysterically.

"Don't worry, Ma. I will handle everything. I have to go now. Mama, call the police and tell them what happened. We will get to you as soon as we can."

"Ok, baby," Lorraine whispered, and hung up the phone.

Charrise put the phone back in her pocket. She turned her eyes from Brianna to Herman who was smiling at Brianna. He was waiting for Ivory to put a bullet in her. Even if he wasn't the one pulling the trigger, he would still get the same joy of seeing it done.

"Who was that?" Brianna asked, noticing the smirk on Charrise's face.

"That was Mommy, and she's alive and safe." Charrise responded.

The smile on Herman's face slowly began to fade. He knew that if Charrise was telling the truth, then his whole plan had just unraveled.

"Look, Ivory, I don't know what's going on, but me and Gwen had an agreement and this bastard dying was part of it. Can you please tell me what changed?" Selena asked while pointing at Herman.

"Yeah well, Selena, I'm a soldier and I just follow Direc—" Ivory was saying before she was cut off by the shining of car headlights through the window of the small home.

"Well Selena, it looks like you can ask her yourself." Ivory continued.

"What's up, Brianna?" Gwen said as she walked into the house, flanked by four other MHB solders. As she walked towards Brianna, the headlights from another approaching car shone on Jonathan's face.

Gwen and Jonathan locked eyes, but before she could react, Jonathan had the gun pointed in her face. Gwen's entrance had been the diversion he needed. The women on the side of Gwen yelled at him to drop the gun as Charrise, Selena, and Brianna instructed him to do the same.

"Whoa, whoa what is going on?" Selena yelled. The distraction that Selena caused gave Gwen the chance to pull her gun. "Gwen, calm down, these are my family."

"Family?" Gwen asked glaring at Jonathan and Brianna. "This is the fool that took over a million from me and murdered my sister right in front of another member. Word is, your big sis is the one that ordered it!" Gwen yelled.

Charrise and Selena turned to look at Jonathan and Brianna.

"What? You robbing and killing people?" Charrise said. "Jonathan! Answer me!"

Jonathan didn't answer Charrise. He didn't move his eyes from Gwen. Charrise ran her fingers through her hair. She looked at Brianna, who was in a war stance. She could see her finger itching to make it to the trigger of the gun in the small of her back. Brianna knew that no matter how much she could have tried to convince Gwen and her crew that she never ordered Jonathan to do anything, there was no way they was going to believe it. She also knew that with the firepower Gwen had behind her, her and Jonathan would be slaughtered.

"Gwen listen, we gotta find a way to resolve this. I can assure you that I had nothing to do with the robbing and killing of you or any MHB member. But I will take responsibility because this is my family. Now I don't know what the fuck is fully going on with my little brother, but we can work this out." Brianna spoke trying to reason with Gwen.

"Fuck this bitch, Bri. She and her crew murdered both my boys. As I see it, I owe her a life for A.J.'s."

"Jonathan, shut the fuck up. If you had not been out here robbing folks your friends would not be dead!" Brianna yelled.

Brianna looked at Gwen with pleading eyes. This would be the one time she would try the mercy role. If it didn't work, it would be time to go all out in a blaze of glory, and Brianna was ready die. She was tired of living with a constant ten thousand pound weight over her head, whether it was jail, stick-up crews, or the rival gangs that were constantly threatening her empire. At that moment, she realized that Brandon was right. Dealing with some bougie and stuck-up black folks was a lot easier than dealing with this life and death style of living she was involved in.

The knock on the door startled everyone inside. The drama that existed inside the house had drawn everyone's attention from the second set of car lights earlier.

Gwen motioned for one of her henchwomen to open the door. The girl slowly opened the door with her gun pointed towards the entrance.

"What up, Gwen?" Eagle said approaching with a black duffel bag.

"Eagle? What the hell you doing here?" she asked.

"Setting this shit straight, Gwen." Eagle said as he threw the duffle bag at her feet. "Let them go, and consider this squared up." Eagle stood between Jonathan and Brianna.

"What, you fucking this bitch while my girl locked up? Nigga!" Gwen yelled. Eagle smiled and shook his head. He handed her his cell phone and motioned for her to listen to the person on the other end.

"What up, bitch? I see you holding shit down." the voice on the other end spoke.

Gwen smiled as the thought of her girl's face entered her mind. "Ni, what's up trick?" she joked back.

"Now on the real, I need you to sit down with girlie and I need you to give the young buck a pass."

"Who are these people to you, Ni?" Gwen asked with a curious look on her face.

"Sis, that's my future sister-in-law." Niya responded.

Gwen's eyes shifted from Eagle to Brianna. She waved for her crew to lower their guns, and nodded to Brianna. "So let's you and I take a walk and talk, and get this shit figured out."

The two ladies walked outside the house and into the blackness of the night. Everyone inside took a seat. They were starting to get nervous when the ladies had been gone for nearly a hour and a half, before they returned, laughing and giggling like two teenagers. Brianna had agreed to give Gwen her blessing with Auntie and to give up all her cocaine and heroin transactions. She would simply deal with weed, and MHB would provide the security and protection for her weed transactions. Both could get what they wanted, Gwen and MHB would have the Carolinas on lock and Brianna would still be getting money and able to fall back and enjoy her new life with Brandon.

Once back in the house, Gwen motioned for her girls to come on.

After talking with Jonathan, Brianna convinced him to ride out with Eagle and check on their mom, and then go to the hospital to check on Kasy and Cowboy. Leaving Brianna, Selena, and Charrise alone in the house with Herman.

"Ok Charrise, I'm not trying to leave you out or treat you like a child, but you sure you want to do this?" Brianna asked with a concerned look on her face. Charrise looked at Herman. This was her father, but when she thought about all the things that he had allowed to happen to her, she couldn't find an ounce of love left in her body towards him.

"Yeah, I'm sure."

Brianna handed her a bottle of Patron and all three started emptying their bottles all over Herman's body while he screamed and tried to wiggle out of his bondage.

"What you crying for now, nigga? I thought you liked liquor?" Brianna asked in a joking manner.

"Maybe he just likes brown, not white liquor." Selena chimed in while laughing.

"Please don't kill me, I will go far way and never come back. I promise... I promise..."

Herman's pleas fell on deaf ears as Brianna struck the matches. She gave one to each of her girls, and all at once, they threw the burning flame sticks on Herman's alcohol drenched body.

Final Chapter

Brianna kissed Cowboy's forehead and hugged her mother.

"You make sure y'all call us okay, to let us know you'll are alright." Lorraine said, hugging Brianna. She touched her stomach and smiled. "I really wish you would stay here, baby, so I can take care of you."

"No, Mommy, you take care of Daddy. I got Brandon, and we will be okay. I just need to get away from here for a while." Brianna squeezed her mother's hand and walked out of the room.

Lorraine had only suffered minor injuries from her ordeal. When the police searched the warehouse where Herman had kept Lorraine captive, they found Tank's corpse and the murder weapon with Herman's prints all over it. Based on the evidence, the police concluded that Herman was planning to set up Cowboy and Brianna for the murder that he had reported to them. Not happy about almost being fooled, and especially eager to distance themselves from the traffic accident that had left Kasy in a coma, the police hurriedly closed the investigation against Brianna and Cowboy and took out a warrant for Herman's arrest. A national manhunt had been launched to bring the killer to justice.

Cowboy was released from the hospital, but still needed help getting around and recovering. Brianna had hired a nurse to help her mother with him. Charrise had promised to help as well, between school and her counseling sessions, which she had resumed.

Brianna and Brandon walked to the white Mercedes truck. She smiled and waved goodbye to her mother.

Brandon got in on the driver's side and kissed her hand. He started up the luxury sedan and drove them off to their new life.

Jonathan checked his reflection in the door of the elevator. He wore a pair of Rock Revival jeans, and a white Gucci button down shirt. His hair was cut low, and his goatee was perfectly manicured, thanks to his boy, Low. He and Gator were finally going to hook up after being apart for several weeks. He had many questions for her, but most of all he just wanted her back in his arms. She had asked him to meet her at this new high-rise apartment building. He wasn't sure exactly what was up with that either. The doors of the elevator opened and Jonathan stepped out onto the plush carpet and walked down the hallway. He stopped at the door with the numbers 1415 on it and pressed the buzzer.

The door slowly opened and a woman smiled weakly at him.

"Hey, I'm Jonathan, I'm here to pick up Gator." Jonathan said, flashing a smile at the woman.

She opened the door and stepped back. Jonathan walked inside the foyer; the woman closed the door, and walked down two steps to the living room. Jonathan saw Gator sitting on the couch. She looked like she had been crying, or was still crying.

"Hey babe, are you ready?" Jonathan said, smiling.

As he began to walk towards the couch, something cold touched the back of his neck.

"You kidding me, right? You going out with this little nigga?" A male voice said from behind Jonathan as he shoved him towards the couch. As Jonathan fell onto the couch, he reached for his gun. As he turned, he fired in the direction of the man.

"Fuck!" the man yelled as he ran towards the door.

Jonathan fired again, hitting him in the other shoulder. Jonathan began to run after him, but Gator stopped him.

"Let him go." Gator said, holding Jonathan's arm.

"Who the fuck was that?" Jonathan said, still looking down the hall.

"That was a fucking ghost." Moon answered.

Made in the USA
Columbia, SC
13 August 2024

40425186R00124